CURSES AND CROSSWORDS

A Spooky Games Club Mystery Book 4

AMY MCNULTY

"Dahlia, you can relax a little. Clutching the car's armrest isn't going to stop us from tumbling off George Washington Bridge."

Dark spots filtered into the edge of my vision as a sense of vertigo wrestled with the jolt of adrenaline making every inch of me tremble. "No, but… it'll stop me… from screaming," I said through clenched teeth.

I'd sworn never to get into a car again a couple of months back.

Now I'd spent the last couple of weeks in Cable's tiny tan death trap darting from literary landmark to literary landmark across the Eastern half of the U.S.

Smart car? More like tiny metal box of compact doom.

Cable reached over and put a hand on my

shoulder, glancing my way. "You're all right. Most people—myself included—find it far scarier to fly up in the air than drive on a bridge, especially on a broomsti—"

"Eyes on the road!" I shouted, and he stiffened, putting both hands on the steering wheel and staring straight forward.

The imposing, gargantuan steel beams and cables made it seem as if this giant road dangling over the Hudson River between Manhattan and New Jersey were held together by strings and glue sticks. I focused on Cable instead. First, it was to make sure he was paying attention to the road as the driver and captain of this perilous voyage, but soon, my shoulders drooped, my neck muscles loosening. Cable Woodward had that effect on me.

Rather built for a professor—or maybe I was just guilty of thinking of professors a certain way—his corded muscles strained against his version of casual attire, a navy cable-knit sweater with a pale pink dress shirt collar peeking out from the top, and cuffs at the edges of his sleeves. Okay, maybe my professor stereotype wasn't too far off. He had round, large glasses, too, and wavy, dark hair that was too wild to tame, making it responsible for the only disheveled aspect of his appearance. Thanks to my panic, no doubt, along with my raised voice, he was clutching the steering wheel, his knuckles white, popping out against his lightly tanned peach complexion.

I bet he wished he'd never invited me along on his two-week trip.

Letting out a deep breath, I peeled my hands off the armrest, one stubborn finger at a time, and leaned back in the seat, settling for clutching the skirt of my plain black dress on my lap instead. It was winter in New York—the first day of winter, actually, though it'd been fairly cold throughout our trip. No snow yet. In fact, it had rained this morning, though now that it *was* cold enough to snow, the precipitation had stopped. To combat the chill, I wore thick, webbed black tights underneath my dress and thigh-high lace-up black boots. I preferred shawls to sweaters, and besides, I could always enchant myself warmer if need be.

Enchantments. Right. *Duh, Dahlia.*

"MLAC." I waved my fingers over my body like a fluttering waterfall. "RAEF ON."

I could always turn my ability to fear back on. It was a survival instinct for a reason. It just got a little out of hand on occasion.

"Ah," I said, leaning back into the seat and closing my eyes. "That's better." I let the smooth turning of the wheels on the pavement, the echoing of the movement over the suspended road below us, wash over me. "Sorry," I said, not opening my eyes. "I didn't mean to snap at you."

Cable let out a chuckle. "You're not wrong. Safety first. Boy, and I thought you were bad on the way *into* Manhattan. But then at least you had all the tall buildings to wonder at, take your mind off things."

My skirt rustled into the air and my eyes popped open in time to see Broomie shoot up from between my feet on the ground and point her brush-head out the window.

I should have been startled at her waking up so suddenly. But I'd enchanted myself to feel no fear.

"How was the nap?" I asked her, running my hand over her bristles and down her shaft. She was flexible, my Broomhilde, which had come in handy in this tiny two-seater car Cable had commandeered for his stay in America. Not that he'd imagined dragging along a witch and her companion broom-stick for any long-distance travel when he'd bought it, I was sure.

Cable started snickering harder. "Are you going to fly up the Empire State Building again, Broomhilde?" We hadn't *just* visited sites of literary significance for Cable's research project. Broomie liked high places. And she was a fan of giant gorillas in black-and-white films. We'd had the movie on at home on occasion.

Broomie whapped her brush head around so fast, I could almost *feel* the glare she sent Cable's way. She'd been on her best behavior this trip. Until I hadn't been able to bring my old-fashioned broomstick I'd been trying to pass off as a walking stick past security for the Empire State Building.

Then, rather than wait for the line to die down so I could cast an enchantment—maybe make me invisible for a moment, so I wouldn't have to mess with anyone and force them to let me through—she'd slipped out of my hands and just shot right up the side of the skyscraper.

She'd waited smugly for us at the top forty-five minutes later. There *had* to have been someone who'd seen her, but Cable had insisted, while looking at his phone, that at least she wasn't "trending," whatever that meant.

Broomie had gotten miffed when she'd realized she hadn't been able to see the King Kong display on the second floor thanks to her shortcut and then she'd waited for me to cast an enchantment on her so she couldn't be seen on the way down.

Cable lifted one hand off the steering wheel in surrender. "You just have to be careful in more crowded cities is all, Broomie. Do you know how many people there are in New York City? Eight point four million. That's…" He went quiet, his fingers moving up and down like he was doing some calculations. "Twenty-eight thousand Luna Lanes. Most towns aren't home to just three hundred."

The mention of Luna Lane made my heart clench.

It had been amazing to stretch my legs for the first time in my life and step outside of the small town in which I'd been born and raised. The "curse" Eithne Allaway had placed on me had only extended to keeping me in town for my protection and *not*, like I'd thought, to making me do the good deeds I'd had to perform every day to keep my skin from turning into stone scales. My aunt had been somewhat wicked, but maybe not *quite* as selfish and evil as I'd always thought of her. Regardless, with her death, it was gone now and I was free to see the world.

I'd started by accompanying Cable on his short trip around to Hannibal, Missouri, Amherst, Massachusetts, and Harlem, Manhattan to take some pictures and do some firsthand research for this American literature research project that was the point of his sabbatical away from his Scotland university for a semester. Maybe some people in my position would have gotten on a plane and never looked back, but…

I was already missing home.

It was almost Christmas. And then my birthday the week after.

I missed my friends. I missed the *quiet* of Luna Lane. How I knew everyone I came across walking down the street.

I cuddled Broomie, wrapping my arms around her shaft and clutching her to my chest. She squirmed a bit at first, putting pressure against me with two little clumps of her bristles to try to wriggle free, but as soon as I let my grip loosen enough for her to stick her brush head back toward the window, she settled in, allowing me my hug.

She'd lived nine lives as different cats before she'd chosen to be a witch's broomstick in her final form. Some habits—like appreciating closeness but not being so much a fan of human cuddles—were hard for her to break.

Cable looked back at me. Overhead, a helicopter's blades thundered above us, the pulsing of the rotors hard to ignore. We didn't get many of those in Luna Lane. Would have made flying up in the sky without being noticed more than a little disastrous. "You doing okay, Dahlia? I didn't mean to minimize your fear of bridges—"

"Cars," I corrected. I leaned my head slightly to get a look at the helicopter, but I couldn't spot it. The chopping sound of its rotors was getting quieter already. Must have moved on from the bridge.

"Cars, yeah. You've been doing so well so far on this trip, though, so I thought the bridge made your anxiety worse. I admit it can be a bit frightening with all this traffic."

"Eyes on the road," I said calmly. I was as relaxed as a mollusk. No tension to my muscles at all.

Cable flicked his gaze back to the road and kept talking. "And sometimes when the weather is rainy and cold like this—ahhh!"

The scream he let out strained his vocal chords

to their limits and his face blanched. Broomie stiffened as straight as she could in the cramped space, her bristles scraping across my cheek. I tilted my head back just a little so she'd avoid scratching my eye.

Meanwhile, our little car was spinning around and around and around on this giant suspension bridge and there were some cars ahead that were bumping together, the metal smashing, glass shattering, headlights spinning around in circles like ours.

Cable was screaming and screaming as he hit the brakes and attempted to correct our course, gripping and turning the steering wheel like someone in a racing movie.

I let out a little giggle. He made for one adorable, nerdy race car driver.

"*Dahlia!*" Cable screamed, his voice scratchy. "Do something!"

Do something? I looked around, my head lolling as we made another spin.

Oh, right.

Crashing. Maybe headed off the bridge. This was what I'd been terrified of.

Terrified of?

I was *supposed* to be terrified of this!

I flung my hands out toward the car's dashboard, focusing on the wheels below us. "POTS!"

The car's wheels stopped turning, but maybe that wasn't such a great idea.

The force of the car sent it skidding, without any sense of control, sliding, sliding, clipping another car and ricocheting backward. Broomie was flying in the opposite direction inside the vehicle as we spun, my broomstick suspended in midair in the cramped car. Then we slammed into the rail in front of the walkway on the bridge.

Cable's shriek died out into panting, gasping breaths.

His hands were still clutching the steering wheel, his face as white as his knuckles now.

I rolled down the window and leaned toward the edge of the bridge. "A few more feet and we'd be dangling off it," I said, as cool as a cucumber. In the air all around us were the squeals of brakes, the endless honking and beeping and the wailing of alarms. Followed by a few more instances of metal and glass crunching.

Cable's jaw dropped and he just stared at me. Broomie was wrapped around his shoulders now, practically tight enough to choke him, her puffed-up bristles shaking like leaves in a hurricane-force gale.

His arm quivering the whole while, Cable peeled one hand off the steering wheel and reached it over to me, touching my thigh. "Maybe you should…" His teeth chattered. "Turn on… your fear?"

Oh, right. The enchantment.

Peering back out across the walkway at the

water below, I turned back to stare at the trembling Cable and Broomie, then looked at the water again.

"Nope. I'm good," I said, letting out a soft sigh as I relaxed back into my seat, as soothing and comfortable as a hammock swaying in a gentle spring breeze.

Chapter Two

"Black ice," said the tow truck driver—one of half a dozen who'd been up to the bridge in the last few hours. "Twelve-car pileup. Haven't seen the like, and not on a bridge, in years. You two are lucky to be standing here." He had a thick Brooklyn accent and seemed mostly unfazed despite his words as he flipped through the papers on his clipboard, his breath white like smog in the frosty air. "No serious injuries in *any* car? That's lucky."

It *had* been luck mostly. I'd been prepared to cast enchantments to save lives if need be, even if I knew erasing memories was still beyond me to do safely, but after doing quick heals for bumps and bruises and aches on both Cable and me and—with Cable's permission—giving him some of that "no fear" enchantment to ride this out with, I'd gone to take a look at the other victims of the icy, unsafe road.

Cuts and bruises and even a broken arm, but Cable had stayed my hand and promised they'd all be okay without me.

It would take months for some of them to heal naturally when it would take *me* just a few words, but he was right.

The last thing I wanted was to make a public display of my abilities for all of the world to see. I'd already been getting enough double takes from the fact that for a while after the accident, I'd been carrying my rough, bristle broom around with me on the icy bridge like it was a hockey stick or something.

She'd been good and stayed stiff to fool all the people around us. For the most part. She'd still been a bit shaky at first, but I'd needed her on her A game for the first hour or so in case we needed to fly because the bridge collapsed or something.

Ha. The bridge collapsing. That would be so scary, wouldn't it? Good thing, thanks to my enchantment, the idea bothered me about as much as eating cereal just a *tad* too soggy.

The mechanic talking to us, still flipping through his papers, was bundled up in a dark, scuffed black down coat complete with puffy hood. It was hard to get a good look at him, though his dark moustache sprinkled with frosted icicles was difficult to miss. Behind him, his similarly puffy-coat-and-pants-outfitted coworker was chaining Cable's wrecked little smart car to the tow truck bed.

Above us, a helicopter flew in circles around the length of the bridge, no doubt broadcasting the incident to the news. The chopping sound was tough to tune out, even when the helicopter retreated closer to Manhattan. Behind the tow truck were flashing lights from police vehicles, ambulances, and even firetrucks, though I wondered at the use of those since there was no fire. Cable explained they came to any big accident, jaws of life and all that, but we didn't have a fire department in Luna Lane. Besides me. And I wasn't there. So I hoped there were no fires when I was gone. Maybe I shouldn't have been gone so long. I sighed, sipping on the coffee in a Styrofoam cup a police officer had offered me. My face screwed up. It tasted like sludge.

Another reason to miss Luna Lane. Faine's brew wasn't to be beat—not even in the fancier cafés we'd tried while on our trip.

This could hardly qualify as drinkable.

"We're from out of town," Cable said, clutching his own coffee and not seeming to mind its sludge-like taste. We both had shiny, foil-like blankets draped over our shoulders from the paramedics that crinkled with every little movement. Mine was especially crinkly because Broomie was currently wrapped around my shoulders under my shawl beneath my foil blanket, and though I'd cast an enchantment to calm her, she still fidgeted in her sleep.

"I can see that," said the guy—Alfie, his nametag read. Behind him, the tow truck bed let out a huge bang, followed by shaking chains, as the bed started righting itself, the smart car in place. Everyone within earshot jumped but Cable and me.

Being afraid made one so jittery. I sipped the sludge just to warm my tongue and gazed at Cable's car. The front and the back were smashed like an accordion. We were lucky the passenger area had been okay.

Wow. We could have been smushed. That ought to have been so scary.

I sipped my sludge again.

Beside Cable on the ground were the two bags we'd packed—there hadn't been room for much in his car's tiny hatchback trunk. One was kind of crumpled awkwardly, the other opened at one corner, the handle broken. I could fix them later when there weren't so many witnesses. Poking out of my bag was a long, black pole made of shiny black onyx that I'd only just fit lengthwise at an angle in Cable's hatchback, some of it slipping under our seats. I could have enchanted it to be smaller or even invisible—Eithne had hidden it away in a playing card somehow—but I hadn't wanted to mess with it. I didn't trust my magic not to break it somehow, and as far as I knew, it was the only weapon I had that could hurt a witch. If necessary.

Which I hoped it wouldn't be.

It got Alfie's attention. His moustache bristled just slightly as he paused to look at it, but he shrugged and didn't ask.

"We were on our way back home," Cable said. I blinked rapidly when he'd said *home*, but I supposed he wasn't about to launch into his life story to this guy.

Cable's home was in Scotland. Where he had a job that was waiting for him—a job he certainly couldn't do in Luna Lane. We had a single school-room that could handle anyone up to high school seniors, but it was currently home to only about forty students of all ages. The few teens we had preferred to commute to Creekdale, though my childhood friends, Faine, Hitesh, and Zashil, had stayed behind with me when we'd been that age. Probably out of pity, since I hadn't been able to leave town. Their high school social lives had been practically squandered because of me. There was a high school in Creekdale with four hundred students. Bigger than the entire town of Luna Lane.

"Well," said Alfie, "you're going to be late now." He chuckled darkly as he flipped through his papers and turned his clipboard to Cable for a signature. Then Alfie pulled a pen out of a pocket on the front of his jacket with finesse despite his puffy gloves. "Heading home for the holidays?"

"Trying to," I said.

Alfie studied us both, his eyes catching on the lump shaking my foil blanket over my shoulders.

"This here piece is totaled, I have to tell you that." The man pointed a thumb over his shoulder just as the tow truck bed settled into place with another loud boom. "Engine's shot. Gas tank busted. You were a hair's breadth away from some *serious* business right there." I nodded, taking in his words and understanding them but not feeling much at all about it. "Cheaper to buy a new car than even begin to *attempt* repairs."

Cable frowned and handed the pen and clipboard back to him. "I don't need another car. I bought this one cheap because I'm in the country for a few months, but I'm headed back overseas at the end of January."

There it was. The confirmation I'd never wanted to ask him for—his sabbatical at an end, his return to Scotland for the new semester.

Alfie gave him a scrutinizing look from above his icicle moustache, as if about to guess which country he was headed to, but he shrugged. "Even more reason to junk it," was all he said.

"But we have to get home," I pointed out.

Alfie tucked his clipboard under his arm. "You could rent a car—"

"No," Cable and I both said as one. I raised an eyebrow at him. He'd never shared my aversion to cars before. It certainly wasn't causing me any anxiety to think about being in a car again, but logically, I knew that was just because of my enchantment.

My brain was calm, but it wasn't foolish enough to forget what had just happened.

Alfie offered us a lopsided grin. "Well, you're in one of the busiest cities on the planet. Plane, bus, train—you've got options." He looked over his shoulder, at his coworker, who nodded at him and started climbing inside the cab of their truck. Turning back to us, he studied our bags. "I could give you a lift as far as Manhattan, but I'm not sure I've got room. There are taxis at the end of the barricade if you'd prefer."

Cable sent one last, sorrowful look toward his little smart car and sighed. "Guess we can do that," he said to me, and I nodded. "Thanks again," he added to Alfie, extending his hand for a shake.

"Sure thing, pal. Careful walking down the street. Still icy."

After breaking down our empty coffee cups and stuffing them into his luggage, Cable grabbed the broken handle of his bag on wheels and slipped my bag over his shoulder, the bottom half of the black onyx pike sticking out behind him like one half of a set of skis. His breath came out in the same white mist as Alfie's and his ears were reddening. I waited until there was no one looking and muttered quietly, "MRAW," gesturing to the both of us.

Cable visibly relaxed and I took the opportunity to fix our bags, too, before muttering, "TLEM ECI, TLEM ECI," over and over again as I cleared the path in front of us.

Nothing too noticeable. If anyone looked over, they'd surely think I was just carefully watching where I was going. With both arms extended in front of me in case of a fall.

"So," said Cable, his breath still coming out like ghostly fog, "regretting coming on this trip with me yet?"

I paused my enchantment casting for just a moment to grab him by the hand, squeezing it. "Not on your life."

Using just the one hand, I kept melting ice with magic until we made it to the end of the bridge. The chill late afternoon air whipped across our cheeks, but my warming magic made it so we didn't even shiver. It'd last for a few hours or until I cast another enchantment to remove it. It differed from enchantment to enchantment, and I was sure it depended on the witch's skill. Though despite Eithne's warning about the hordes of wicked witches who would be out for my life, I hadn't met another one besides her and my late mom yet.

Still, I wasn't taking too many chances. That was what the giant onyx pike was for.

Not that I was in a rush to kill any more witches.

Thinking about my role in Eithne's death made me queasy enough. Even if she'd orchestrated it, even if I truly believed she would have followed through with her threat to kill my friends one by one if that was what it would have taken to get me to end her and break the enchantment keeping me in Luna Lane the first thirty years of my life.

"We'll make it home for Christmas," he promised me.

There it was. That word again. Home.

Biting my lip, I just squeezed his hand back. I couldn't bring myself to talk about it.

"Do you want to spend the night in town and head out tomorrow?" Cable asked.

I shook my head. Ever since Eithne had told me the money I'd enchanted out of my mom's inter-dimensional vault had been from her, and that it was all old Irish pound, I hadn't been able to bring myself to bring any along. Besides, this world ran on credit and debit cards and smartphone appy things I didn't understand. So far, it had all been on Cable's dime. And at this point, I was eager to get home.

"Let's get out of here tonight if we can."

Cable smiled at me and nodded in agreement.

My heart fluttered. We hadn't yet talked about, well, that *true love* thing. Kissing him had broken my good-deed curse, which had really been some kind of genetic issue I'd inherited from my gargoyle father.

I didn't fully understand it, but what I *was* more focused on—to an obnoxious degree—was that it was kissing Cable that had made my stone scales vanish. I looked at my left forearm, at the smooth skin peeking out from under my foil blanket and shawl. There'd been stone scales there once, in what had looked like a tattoo at first glance, even if the hard, silvery skin had had the same properties as stone.

Cable and I hadn't even kissed since.

He'd been as embarrassed about the discovery of what had cured me as I had.

Or so I thought. I was… too scared to talk about any of this, and how our burgeoning romance would be impacted when he went back home.

I hadn't decided yet if I would follow him to Scotland.

True love or not, whatever my blood may have thought of Cable, I was taking it slow. We were still just getting used to the idea of dating.

Finally, beyond the barricade set up to block out traffic, we nodded at the woman directing traffic and headed for the line of yellow cars with checkered stripes and little signs reading "taxi" on top of them about a block away from where all of the rest of the traffic was turning around.

Cable hailed one, and I stroked softly-snoring Broomie through the layer of my foil blanket and shawl as Cable and the cabbie went around to his trunk to load up our bags. "Where to?" he asked us, and Cable looked at me.

"Bus, plane, or train?" he asked.

"No bus," I said, that logic pounding through that it would involve being on America's highly packed roadways. This wasn't like Luna Lane, where one car went by the street every few hours.

Broomie stirred underneath her covers atop my shoulders, poking her head up, making it seem like I'd just grown a four-inch-high singular shoulder pad. The cabbie, a stout man with a heavy Middle Eastern accent, stared straight at my shoulder, his misty breath suddenly going still.

I pushed her down—gently, but quickly. It was the mention of planes. She'd probably love to fly on one, despite the fact that she could fly on her own, but the reason I'd nixed the idea in the first place when we'd been planning our little trip, besides inconvenience since Cable had had multiple stops on his itinerary, was I wasn't sure there'd be room for her in a carry-on. I'd have to enchant her invisible and hope she didn't get overly excited about looking outside and give us away somehow. Like by scraping against the window with her little excited clumps of bristles.

Enchantments at thirty-five-thousand feet above sea level were something I hadn't yet attempted.

"Train station," I offered and Cable, one hand on his hip, nodded.

The cabbie glanced from Cable to me and back, his dark eyebrow twisting up in confusion.

We weren't exactly dressed for the weather. Cable had brought a coat, but it was still in his bag. With my warming enchantment and all the chaos of what we'd been through, we'd forgotten to take it out.

"Which station?" the cabbie asked.

And I realized in a city this size, there couldn't be just one.

"Whichever one will get us to Chicago," I suggested. I turned to Cable. "We can get someone to pick us up from there." It'd be a bit of a drive, but just a couple of hours. Faine had a car, and so did the Mahajans. They were bound to be busy, but they'd understand in this case. They were their own bosses, too, so they could *probably* manage some time off. Too bad they were also pretty strict bosses—of themselves.

"Both stations have trains to…" started the cabbie. He was staring at the "lump" on my shoulder. Broomie had moved a little.

"Never mind," said the cabbie, quickly spinning on his heel. His back stiffened as if steeling himself, eager to get this over with or trying to dismiss whatever flights of fancy his mind had led him on. Probably both. "I'll take you to Penn. Speedtracks runs to Chicago."

Cable opened the door and held it for me. I slid inside and he shut it, then walked around to the other side.

The cabbie adjusted the rearview mirror, the engine of the car running idle as a wave of heat blasted inside the vehicle from the cab's air vents.

Cable opened the door to his side.

Then, with a rush of force, my pulse went into overdrive, black spots overtaking my vision as the interior of the cab seemed to be closing in on me.

I shrieked at the top of my lungs, the memories of spinning on the black ice, of hitting another car, of almost tumbling off the side of the bridge all catching up with me.

My screaming prompted Broomie to shoot up, outstretching her body and unfurling from around my shoulders. Her brush head peeked out from beneath my foil blanket and shawl, her bristles shaking in time with my bloodcurdling fear.

The cabbie said something in a foreign language, opened his door, and took off, running down the sidewalk and around the block, the cab still running.

Chapter Three

"I'm sorry," I said for the millionth time as we approached the escalators leading down into Penn Station.

Cable smirked. "You don't have to apologize to me. I wish you could apologize to that poor cab driver."

I'd looked for him after my nerves had settled. He'd been long gone. Cable and I had settled for turning off his vehicle for him and he'd ripped a page out of his notepad so I could write an apology and stick it on his front seat. Cable had added the last of his cash—a hundred-dollar bill—beneath it and I'd promised to pay him back at some point. I hoped the cab driver came back and found it before anyone else did.

We'd walked a few more blocks before hailing another cab—out of the area where someone might have heard me scream—and asked the new driver to take us to the station.

I'd clutched my bag against my chest the whole ride, biting my tongue to keep myself from shrieking again at the rather slow ride to the station that wasn't at all in the same league as spinning out of control on a giant bridge. We were constantly stopping for traffic lights and pedestrians darting out in front of us, for one thing. I wasn't going to enchant my fear away this time, though. It had made the situation bearable for a time, but my slow reflexes had almost gotten us killed—and besides, I knew now from regrettable experience that if I wasn't paying close attention, my fear would come back and hit me all at once and I'd wind up shrieking and hyperventilating at the entirely wrong moment.

Nope. Not doing that again anytime soon.

A throng of people moved along the sidewalk where the second cabbie had dropped us off, brushing past us as they headed to and away from the escalators. Many were in business suits and woolen coats, but quite a few dragged suitcases behind them. Everyone was more bundled up than we were. But somehow, despite that and the long onyx shaft sticking out of Cable's bag, the looks directed our way were more of the "move, already" variety if I had to describe it. Dismissive annoyance rather than idle curiosity.

Maybe it wouldn't be so hard for a witch or another paranormal creature to blend in with everyone in a giant city after all. I wondered why so many of us congregated in small towns… Then I figured maybe even New Yorkers would stop and do a double take if I soared over their heads on Broomie's back.

"Shall we?" Cable asked, gesturing toward the descending escalator. His hand whapped against a man's chest, and the guy muttered something like, "Watch it" and moved on his way. Cable pulled his hand back and clutched it in front of his chest as if wounded.

Maybe his mom hadn't taken him to lots of big cities during his worldwide travels in his youth.

"Let's go," I said, taking his hand. Broomie stirred beneath my shawl—we'd ditched the crinkly blankets on the rim of the nearest trashcan after the incident with the first cabbie; hopefully, someone in need would find them before they were collected—as we headed to the escalator.

The escalator. Yes, I'd been on some during our travels. Well, the little sightseeing we'd done here in Manhattan.

It was all about timing.

A short man in a dark woolen coat let out an audible sigh and brushed past me, practically leaping onto the escalator step as it kept turning and turning.

"Dahlia?" Cable asked.

"Three, two…" I started. Then I ran, dragging him with me. "One!" I landed perfectly on the nearest step as it appeared and turned back to look at him smugly.

He stumbled a little on the step above me. I probably shouldn't have yanked him on here with me.

"Excuse me," said a woman behind Cable. She was trying to squeeze past him on one side and I realized with a start as I looked above and below me that people just riding the escalator down were all sticking to one side, leaving the other side open for people rushing down the stairs.

Rushing down *moving* stairs. Were they reckless? Or just really well coordinated?

Cable leaned back against the edge of the escalator and let the woman pass.

She seemed about my age. Smooth, dark tawny complexion and a perfectly round face, silky, black hair pulled back into a tight bun behind her head, held together by two hair sticks. She looked to be wearing a uniform of some kind, a crisp pantsuit like a stewardess, a nametag over her breast reading, "Lien." But she moved so fast past us, offering us a flittering smile, it was a mystery why I'd managed to take in so much detail as I had. She reached the bottom of the escalator, disappearing beyond my sight into the crowd, dragging a very small bag on a set of wheels behind her. So small, I wondered why anyone had bothered adding an adjustable handle and wheels. It was either for an overnight trip or a work purse of some sort.

She probably did work on one of the trains, now that I thought about it.

"Dahlia," said Cable, snapping me back to the moment. We were approaching the bottom of the stairway. "You don't have to cou—"

"Three, two," I said aloud, "one!" I jumped off my step and onto the bottom.

Behind us, a couple of teenage girls let out little giggles and moved past us into a nearby underground drug store. I stopped and stared, open-mouthed. There were *underground* stores in this city? Was there a whole second city underground?

"Come on," said Cable, his eyes sparkling brightly as he looked over at me. "Unless you need anything before we go?"

I shook my head. It was just about dinner time and I imagined we'd need to grab something to eat before we left, but I wanted to make sure we set our plans before I worried about any of that. If we hadn't gotten into that accident, we would have been stopping for dinner somewhere in Pennsylvania or Ohio by now.

We made our way through the crowds. Some people were *running* around the other people, while many more people just… stood there. Staring up. A board above their heads listed names of train destinations, I assumed, about a quarter of which had a track number lit up beside them, the rest blank.

Cable let go of my hand to stare up at the name of the train line over the ticket counter. "I don't think they go long-distance," he said, peering around and noting the pointing signs leading to other train tracks. "Ah. Let's head this way."

Almost as if they'd been listening to him, about half of the crowd gathered sparked to life, bending down to grab suitcases and shopping bags and luggage on wheels and rushing forward to another set of escalators. A new track number flashed next to the words "Long Beach" on the sign the rest of the people were still staring at. A number of them stirred to life and funneled into the matching track number over a door leading down.

"Rush hour," Cable said loudly.

Broomie shivered a little under my shawl and I pet her through the wool. It was a bit much for a couple of gals used to the small-town quiet life. Sensory overload. Someone slammed against me as he made his way to the door attracting the crowd.

"Watch it!" Cable shouted at him, but the man with his suitcoat over one arm totally ignored us.

I laughed. It was like an echo of the guy who'd yelled at Cable for accidentally smacking him. He was an honorary New Yorker already.

Cable reddened. "This way."

I followed him past more stores and restaurants —underground! People were dining out underground!—and through another set of doors, which took us to what felt like a station within the station, an entirely different line of tickets with the Speed-tracks logo emblazoned everywhere overhead.

Cable paused in front of a computer screen on the wall with a list of city names. These ones were more recognizable than the commuter train destinations we'd passed before. Denver, Atlanta, Los Angeles…

"Chicago," said Cable. He nodded. "Twenty-one hours. An overnight."

"It takes twenty-one hours even in a train?" I asked. I'd expected another day on the road before this, probably stopping for the night somewhere in Ohio or Indiana, but I'd figured trains had to be faster. It wasn't like they had to deal with the same kind of traffic. They had their own little train-track roadways.

"No high-speed rail in this country," Cable said. "But it's fine. Look, we can get a sleeper car."

I wondered how much that would cost. But once I managed to exchange Eithne's Irish pounds, I'd pay him back. At least for my half, if not more.

He didn't have to bring me along on this trip, after all, and he was now out a car he'd probably planned to sell when he moved back to Scotland.

Yeah. I should probably pay him more than half.

It wasn't like I had big plans for my somewhat wicked aunt's money.

"That's fine," I said. "I'm just surprised is all." I wondered briefly if I could teleport us back, but nah —I'd only performed that enchantment under duress and it had been a few feet, not almost a thousand miles. "We'll still be back before Christmas. I'll wait here with the bags."

I helped Cable get his arm out of my bag and leaned against the pillar, shifting aside to let other travelers access the information on the screen. Stroking Broomie through my shawl, I closed my eyes, taking a quick moment to rest, despite the endless buzzing of conversations and the loud rumbling of trains pulling into and out of the station.

"Oh, look at that, Sally, Dora!"

I opened my eyes to find an elderly woman taking hold of a pair of cats-eye glasses that had been dangling on a silver chain around her neck and placing them on her face, making her bulbous brown eyes seem almost three times their size. She reminded me starkly of Milton Woodward, Cable's uncle and my neighbor, and how he kept his late wife's glasses around his neck much of the time, even if he didn't need them himself. She was about a head shorter than me—though I was pretty tall— with wispy, white hair and a pink cardigan that matched her fuzzy, bright pink skirt. She looked as out-of-place amidst all the businesspeople and travelers as I did. Maybe more so.

Another two women about her age meandered up behind her to peer at the screen beside me. Both were taller than the first, and a little less shaky. Wrinkled but carrying herself with the air of someone decades younger, the tallest one with the dark brown complexion and white hair cropped almost to her scalp nodded at the screen. She had thick, green eyeshadow and long, bright green nails and wore an elegant forest green pantsuit. "Why, how fun!"

The third woman, short and curvy, wore a flowery, long-sleeved dress and clutched a leather wallet to her chest. It seemed handmade, like something someone might have bought at a craft fair, and was sealed with a wooden button and a bit of elastic. She bounced a little in place, her wavy, unnaturally red hair so stiff, it didn't even move along with her. "And here we were worried about not having enough to do on this long, overnight trip to Chicago."

That got my attention. I peered around the corner to see what they were looking at. The list of train schedules had changed to an advertisement, or announcement, I supposed.

Book a ride on the Speedtracks Overnight Express to Chicago December 21st and compete in our crossword puzzle holiday event! Free to enter with purchase of train ticket. Winner wins refunded passage and a $1000 cash prize!

A crossword holiday event? Did trains usually do such things?

"Get your dictionary out, Mabel," said the tallest woman to the one with glasses. "One of us is going to win that prize!"

Mabel fished through the oversized tote bag over her shoulder and pulled out an actual dictionary. Paperback, sure, but thick nonetheless. The woman traveled with a dictionary?

Then again, I traveled with an onyx witch-killing pike and a sentient broomstick.

"Do you like crossword puzzles, dear?" asked the redheaded one.

The tallest one nudged her. "Don't talk to strangers in the big city, Dora. They don't like it."

"No, it's fine," I said, remembering I was still petting Broomie, so I clutched my hands together in front of me. "Besides, I'm not… I'm not from here. Small town girl."

The tall one I assumed to be Sally drew back, resting those long fingers on her collarbone. "You don't say. You're as glamorous as a city girl."

My cheeks flushed. She was just being nice, surely. I was wearing basic witchy attire, minus my pointed black conical hat with a purple belt over the brim. That was stuffed as small as it would go into the bottom of my bag. I thought even in a city as packed to the brim with a variety of people as New York, it might have drawn too much attention. Maybe I hadn't been right about that.

"Nonsense," said Dora, gesturing at me with her wallet. It was overly big and rectangular, like a letter wallet. "Sweet little pretty thing like her? Small town honey, through and through."

I laughed nervously. I still wasn't the best at making new friends. Oh, but she'd asked me a question before the conversation had gone off on a tangent. "I enjoy crosswords," I said, suddenly getting a little excited at the idea of something extra to do during the long voyage home. "In fact, I'm part of a Games Club back home." Why was I telling them this? But they all three seemed to be impressed, nodding and following along.

"How nice!" Dora said, clapping her wallet against her chest.

"Though I can't say I'm particularly good at crossword puzzles or anything." I cleared my throat. I didn't want them to think I'd been bragging.

"Nonsense," said Mabel. She tapped her temple with her big dictionary. "Anyone can learn their vocabulary, their trivia. All it takes it a little know-how and determination."

"It'll take significantly more than that." A deep, baritone voice that echoed out into the big space almost like an opera singer drew all of our attention. The sign behind Mabel had changed back to displaying the train schedules.

A man stood there—probably late middle-aged. He had a thin moustache that had been waxed into swirls at both ends and glasses so small and round, they barely covered his wide, blue eyes. He was pale, his hair a sort of white-blond, a small goatee in the shape of an upside-down triangle at the point of his pronounced chin. Atop his head was a faded brown bowler hat that perfectly matched his suit and made his somewhat wan rose complexion seem a little washed out.

Under one arm he carried a black folio bag, the other dragging a rather large roller suitcase behind him.

"Ladies," he said, nodding his head at all four of us in turn. He had some kind of hard-to-place British accent—or was it Irish? It might have been Welsh. "I do apologize, but I overheard you speaking about crossword puzzles. Do you intend to enter the Speedtracks' holiday event on the train to Chicago?"

"Why, yes," said Mabel, adjusting her glasses as if to get a better look at him. "We're headed to Chicago anyway. To see family." She nodded at her companions, who gave her wide smiles back, and then shook her dictionary at the man. "And I can crossword with the best of them."

The man let out a pinched, restrained laugh. His Adam's apple above his tight, high, white collar bobbed somewhat, drawing attention to the long, thin dark red scar that crossed the lump in his throat and vanished somewhere beneath the collar. A glistening silver pen cap clipped a breast pocket on his light brown suitcoat beside a dull, black handle. A letter opener? I hoped it wasn't an actual weapon. "Forgive me. But I *am* the best of them. Rhys Wallaya Aloveius, a champion cruciverbalist across the Continent and North America. And I will walk away with this prize to add to my collection." He looked around the station, at the throng of people headed here and there, and sneered. "Otherwise, I wouldn't have found myself on this train to begin with."

"You're riding the train *just to* compete in this event?" Sally asked. She could sneer just as good as him.

"Of course. There is no crossword puzzle competition I will not hear about. And I do not worry that you shall provide much competition, but it would be remiss of me to allow you to nurture false hopes." He used the hand still clutching the portfolio bag to tip the brim of his hat at us. "Now if you'll excuse me." He walked away toward the platforms, the rolling of his suitcase loud enough to echo out above the sounds of everything else. One of his wheels wobbled, the weight of the suitcase seemingly too much.

Sally arched her eyebrows and Mabel muttered something unintelligible under her breath—but the approximate content of it was hard to miss. Dora shrugged her shoulders. "City folk, I tell you."

"I don't think he's from New York—" I started, but the ladies were already speaking amongst themselves, headed back to a pile of bags unattended some feet away by the wall. Their luggage seemed a scattered mix of plain and flowery bags and a copious amount of tote bags, as well as paper shopping bags.

"Good luck in the event, dear," said Mabel, turning my way.

"You, too," I offered.

She shook her dictionary above her head. When the women reached their eclectic collection of bags, Dora sat down a small velvet purple trunk, complete with a lock on it, her wallet tucked tenderly on her lap.

Broomie chirruped softly beneath my shawl.

"Do you know them?"

I jumped.

Cable stood behind me with two tickets in one hand.

"Oh. Them? No, I… They just started talking to me." I smiled as Cable tucked our tickets into the front pocket of his folio bag. "There's apparently going to be a crossword puzzle event on the train ride. First prize is a ticket refund—and a thousand dollars."

"I know." Cable's teeth gleamed. He knew? "I *did* run into someone I knew. Clear across the Atlantic, of all places." He looked over his shoulder and I shuddered to think of that Rhys man being his acquaintance, even if he had seemed rather academic. But he waved to another man entirely. A portly man with glasses in a tweed suit, with thinning, dark hair grown on one side into a rather obvious combover over his shiny, pale brown scalp. He waved back at Cable.

"Bedwyr!" Cable called. "This is my… my girlfriend, Dahlia."

I blinked.

And blinked again.

Girlfriend? Of course. My blood had responded to him as if he were my true love. But part of me had wondered if maybe that *hadn't* been the actual reason his kiss had made my stone scales fade away. I was just basing that idea off of Eithne's throwaway comment, after all. And we hadn't really *talked* about it, and—

"Nice to meet you, Dahlia," said the man as he approached. He extended his hand out for a shake and I took it, finding his palm rather clammy, but his smile genuine and infectious. "Bedwyr Hamdi. Former colleague at the university Cable teaches at." He *did* speak with a more definable posh London accent, though I might have expected him to have a Scottish accent. They had a lot of transplant professors at Cable's place of work, I supposed. Bedwyr cocked his head as he straightened his bowtie. "You look familiar. What did you say your last name was?"

"I didn't," I said.

"Pop—" started Cable, but I elbowed him in the stomach and he cut himself off with an *oof.* I didn't know how many people would recognize my last name, but I wasn't exactly eager to spread it around. Based on the family motto—Latin for "May the earth rest lightly on you"—I wagered my family wasn't exactly known for its benevolent past. I wondered why Mom had never changed her name, if even Eithne had. Though I'd known they'd had different fathers. Perhaps "Poplar" wasn't their mother's last name.

"Pope," I said, rolling with the sound Cable had managed to utter.

"Pop Pope?" Bedwyr asked, cocking his head. Then again, the "ah" in "pop" wasn't that much like the "oh" in "pope" at all. Whoops. Wrong choice.

"Just 'Pope,'" I said, doing my best to not to clench my jaw.

Bedwyr nodded, stroking his chin. "Nice, strong Scottish name. Ever get to Scotland? That where you met Mr. American Literature Professor here?"

"No," I said, tapping a finger against my elbow. This story was spinning out of control.

"Hmm, well… I'll think of where I've seen you yet. Or perhaps some of your Scottish kin." He winked. Considering the picture Eithne had painted of my grandmother, the witch queen, I hoped he'd never met any of my "kin." Unless they'd been on my father's side. I wasn't sure how gargoyle golem family trees worked, but from what little Eithne had explained, my father himself seemed kind enough.

Maybe I'd go looking for him someday. But it'd all been too soon to process everything I'd learned —I hadn't even told anyone about the witch royal blood in me—to think about that.

I'd have to summon Eithne's spirit and ask her for more details first.

"Made head of the department yet?" Bedwyr teased Cable.

"Oh, no, I..." Cable glanced over at me, an elbow bent awkwardly as he clutched the back of his head. "I'm not sure I want that."

"Ah, haven't discussed it yet with the ball and chain?" Bedwyr nudged Cable and I blanched at being addressed as such.

"Well, no," said Cable, his ears reddening, "but I'm fairly new. Sam has a few years left in him yet."

"Not at the rate he packs away those neeps and tatties," joked Bedwyr.

Cable laughed nervously. "Well, I meant at the university, but..."

"I only taught there for a semester," Bedwyr explained. "Found a more challenging calling than dealing with all those stuffy suits."

"Oh?" I asked, wondering if he thought of my *boyfriend* as a "stuffy suit."

He tapped the briefcase he'd been clutching to his side. "I do a lot of traveling setting up these kind of puzzle events. Crossword ones are particularly popular. It's my Puzzle Society in London that's sponsoring this holiday train event with Speedtracks."

Ah. That explained how Cable had found out about it. Though it was still quite a coincidence that had led him to the same train we were about to board.

"We're in a Games Club," said Cable, wrapping

an arm around my waist as he practically bounced on his feet and beamed with pride. "So I hope we can still compete—even if I do know you."

Bedwyr laughed. "Why not? Do you think I'd honestly give you some kind of advantage just because we used to lecture two halls down from one another? Oh, no, my fine friend. You're on your own." He winked. "Let me see what this Games Club has done to finetune that scattered brain of yours."

Scattered brain? Cable was one of the smartest people I knew. He'd helped me solve a mystery more than once. He and all of my friends, but…

An announcement rang out overhead. "Speedtracks train Overnight Express to Chicago. Now boarding Track 6."

Bedwyr jolted upright. "If you'll excuse me," he said, jutting his chin at Cable and me in turn. "I do hope you'll join the event. See you inside!"

He, along with a throng of the people gathered all around us, came to life, collecting their bags and headed to the track labeled "6." Cable bent to grab our bags and Broomie poked her brush head upward, but I gently patted her back down as I looked around to see if anyone noticed. The three older ladies off to see family chattered as they passed, their eclectic collection of bags hanging off their arms or otherwise dragging behind them. I only just caught a glance of that pompous Rhys fellow as he vanished down the escalator, practically the first to arrive on the track. I did a double take as my gaze then fixed on a group of three large, burly men, together carrying a human-sized trunk and moving slowly but steadily toward the escalator. They looked a lot alike, and they all hid under page boy caps tilted downward, so I couldn't get a good look at their faces. Their tall frames were hard to miss, though, even if all three wore identical navy wool coats that came down to their knees. The one in the back held the back end of the brown trunk above him like a bodybuilder—and he definitely had the body to show for it—while the two in front carried the front over one shoulder like a pair of pallbearers. Their slow gait reminded me of a funeral procession, too.

"Shall we?" Cable asked.

I spun on my heel. "Oh, yes, of cou—"

"Wicked!" A child's small voice carried over the noise as a shiny black scalp poked into sight around Cable.

"Smooth," added another, this one slightly lower-pitched, though still clearly a child. The top of this head was equally black and shiny, though the hair was shorter and a pale white ear drew my eye like a beacon in the night. Two sets of pale white hands popped up now, too, all caressing the shaft of the black onyx pike poking out of my bag over Cable's shoulder.

"Don't touch that!" I shouted, rushing around Cable to get a better look.

Two children of equal heights pulled back as if struck at the sight of my furrowed brow and my hands on my hips. The girl had long pigtails that reached her waist and a slate-gray, plain dress, under which she wore black tights that ended in furry black boots. The boy was also decked out in all gray, a sweater and a pair of shorts—despite the weather—under which he'd also worn black leggings that ended in black boots. They both had almost identical heart-shaped faces, swaths of brown freckles over their noses, and wide, bright blue eyes resting over deep purple bags that reminded me with a start of a vampire's bloodbag donor who'd given a bit too much blood. Aside from the ashy paleness of their skin and the violet of those eyebags, the blue was the only bit of color on either one of them.

They reminded me of the impish pair of twins in Draven's cursed—*enchanted*—board game. Dreadful and Decadent Darling.

"Hey, kids," Cable said, his face warming despite the fact that two very strange, otherworldly children were practically hanging off of him. "Are you lost?"

"January! August!" shouted a shrill woman. The clomp, clomp, clomp of a pair of high heels drew my attention to a woman—beautiful but twisted somehow, like she'd been drawn over with a water-color brush and the colors had all dripped together to produce some kind of warped aestheticism. She marched straight for the kids from the ticket counters, juggling two bags on rollers behind her. On one bag I noticed what could best be described as a circular purple hat box, only there was a lock to keep anyone from prying around inside of it.

She *did* wear quite a hat. "Children! I told you to stay put!"

She stopped right behind them, panting and leaning back on one of the roller suitcases in all her strange glory. She also was pale white and had black hair, slicked into a fashionable bun at the side of her head. Her purple hat was wide-brimmed and decorated with feathers and mesh that hung down over half her face, and her pencil skirt and matching suitcoat were in the same color, a sort of washed-out lavender that could almost be construed as gray. Her legs, crossed at the ankle as she sat on her own suitcase, displayed mesh black tights that ended in black, laced-up boots with heels that seemed like a shorter version of the pair I was currently wearing myself. She shared her children's scarily bright blue eyes and she fanned herself with a gloved hand.

"Are you all right?" Cable asked, letting go of his own roller suitcase and gently sliding my bag back to the ground before rushing over to her.

The children's eyes lit up as they bent down to look closer at my onyx pike. Fortunately, they couldn't see the pointed end of it.

Right. I'd probably need to make it invisible if I was going to pass any security checks with it, even if it did look like it could just be a shiny… metal… walking stick?

Walking sticks had been my go-to a lot on this trip, and I'd met pretty much no one who'd bothered to use one. Maybe it was more of a witch thing and canes were what the normies used if they needed support.

"Oh, thank you," said the woman, brightening. I was already leaning down and pulling my bag out of the children's reach. Their hands were hovering over the pike as if eager to stroke it once more.

"Leave that be," I said. "It's dangerous."

Wrong thing to say.

"Dangerous?" The girl reached out toward it again. "Wicked!"

I shoved the bag behind me with my boot. "EKIP ELBISIVNI," I murmured under my breath. I checked over my shoulder. Good. It wasn't visible any longer, and I hadn't messed up and turned the whole bag or part of the pillar behind me invisible, too.

"What did you say?" The boy stiffened and stared at me.

"Huh?" I asked. "Nothing."

"You spoke some other language," said the girl, slapping her knees with both palms excitedly. "No, you spoke like—like some wicked language!"

They'd *heard* that?

"Children!" called their mother. Her long-fingered hand with gray polished nails clutched

Cable's arm. I frowned. "Please stop bothering the nice lady."

Both kids jumped to their feet and started chanting, holding one another's hands. "KIP IVNI!" That wasn't the enchantment I'd used, but it was clearly their own interpretation of it. "KIP IVNI!"

"Twins," said their mother, letting out a harried chuckle. She leaned on Cable to stand straight again. "Thank you," she told him, patting him dearly, as if he were an old friend.

There was something about her familiarity, her strange sense of fashion, her startlingly bright eyes.

Eithne. For some reason, she reminded me of Eithne.

A… witch?

My chest squeezed as my breath went still. No, it couldn't be.

Chapter Four

"January," the woman said, finally letting go of my boyfriend and gesturing for her children to come to her. The girl dropped her brother's hands and responded first. "August," she added, then the boy came as well.

She clutched one child on each side of her, and they clung to her abdomen. They had to be at least ten or so, a bit old to cling to their mother like that, but these kids were anything but normal.

Could they be… the children of a witch?

Were there any male witches? Eithne hadn't mentioned any. But there was a lot Eithne hadn't mentioned.

I should have stayed home. Summoned that wicked aunt of mine, gotten some answers. I knew my mom was beyond my reach now, but Eithne still had so much to answer for.

But I'd been so excited to put it all behind me. And now I was far from home, without access to any potions, my potions book, or anything. All I had was my intuition, my own skill, and that black onyx pike.

At least a part of me had been prepared to face potential danger on this trip.

"We're headed to Chicago," said the mother, her dazzling white smile clashing with the dark purple of her lipstick. "You?"

"Yes," said Cable, clearly oblivious to the strangeness of this family. Or was I just being paranoid? This was New York, after all. There were so many normies here, a number of them had to be eccentric. It was just a matter of probability. "Headed home for the holidays after a couple of weeks on a trip." Cable wrapped an arm around me and squeezed. Broomie fluttered at the movement, poking just the smallest tip of a bristle out from under my shawl.

Both January and August immediately zeroed in on it. Of course. Their eyes looked about to roll out of their sockets.

"Cable Woodward," said my professor boyfriend, all smiles. Right. His "no fear" enchantment probably hadn't worn off naturally yet. That would explain a lot, actually. "And this is my girlfriend, Dahlia."

"Oh, how sweet," said the woman. The kids were squirming out from under her grip now, bending at the knees and walking over like waddling ducks as they tried to peer up my shawl. "Um…" I said, taking a step back, smoothing down my shawl while I was at it.

"Odessa Grimm," said the woman, oblivious to her children waddling at me and holding out a bony hand for us both to shake. I did, patting Broomie beneath the shawl, half out of habit and half to offer some comfort in the face of these unsettlingly strange children.

Odessa pulled her children back to either side of her. "And these are my twins, January and August. We're off to Chicago on some *very important business*." She looked unsettlingly at me and then Cable when she said that, her expression so bright, it seemed strained. "Right?" she asked her kids, hugging them to her.

"Yes," they said in unison, but their eyes were focused on me. Entirely. Unblinking. "Very important business."

"Please board the Speedtracks Overnight Express to Chicago on Track 6. Departing in five minutes," said an announcement overhead.

Cable, Odessa, and I jolted as one, scrambling for the bags.

"Children, please, each of you grab a roller bag," Odessa said.

I took my own bag and draped it over my shoulder, accidentally whapping Cable in the back with the invisible pike.

"Sorry," I said.

He patted his behind. "I was about to ask if you'd dropped it," he said quietly. "But good thinking on the invisibility. Might raise too many questions."

"Where's the shiny black stick?" There was one of those very questions. January was over by my bag, reaching for the pike, which *was* there and she would know that if she managed to touch it…

I jumped back, and the pike struck the pillar behind me, ringing out, only there was so much noise and bustle, I wasn't sure anyone would notice.

January and August went still, then exchanged a look, then turned back to me.

Of course they'd notice.

"January, please!" said Odessa.

That was my cue to hurry along, too. I dove in with the rest of the crowd scrambling for Track 6.

"That was close," I said to Cable as he trotted up next to me and I did my "three, two, one" count-down to jump on the escalator.

Cable nodded. "Next train for Chicago doesn't leave until tomorrow morning. We're lucky we got here when we did."

Oh, that. I didn't think he'd noticed the Grimm twins' overly observant behavior.

I shuddered. Even their family name seemed like a guise for hiding witchy secrets.

Once I reached the bottom of the escalator and made a jump for the landing, I swung my bag around and clutched it to my front, to keep a better

eye on when the pike might be in danger of whapping anything. Not that I could see it, of course. As I
wandered around the platform, most of the people
around me headed for specific open train car doors,
as if they knew where they were going. It was a train
with at least twenty-five cars, if not more. Sleek
silver with wide windows every few feet.

Cable pulled our tickets out of his bag's front
pocket and unfolded them. "I think we're in
Car 12…"

"Coming through!" shouted a harried, deep
voice. I barely had time to whip myself and my bag
around as a man in a uniform rushed by, likely just
missing coming into contact with my invisible pike.
He wore a familiar uniform… I'd seen a similar one
on that woman on the escalator, only he had a blue
conductor's hat on to match. A trim, black beard on
his dark complexion, his whole appearance was
impeccable, his eyebrows drawn together as he
approached the front of the train.

A man in the engine in a similar uniform
hopped off to greet him. "Conductor Zapatero.
Engine ready."

"Check it again, Bill."

"But, sir—"

"*Again*, Bill. Nothing preventable happens on my
watch."

They both disappeared back into the engine car.

"Dahlia," called Cable. "Come on!" He was
wheeling his suitcase toward the car labeled "12."

The train let out a whistle that I could only assume meant it was about to go. As I scurried after Cable, the platform nearly empty now, the Grimm family made their way to Car 13 just beyond us, the kids sparing a glance my way every few minutes.

Cable lingered in Car 12's open doorway, peering out at me. "Hurry!"

The train whistled again.

Broomie stirred beneath my shawl, but my hands were full and I couldn't nudge her to lie down. Her head popped out from under the shawl just as I leaped across the gap and onto the train.

January's mouth dropped open on the platform right outside of Car 13's open door, a long, lanky hand reaching outward to yank her inside the train.

That wasn't good news.

"You hungry yet?" Cable asked. We were inside our sleeper car and the train had pulled out of Manhattan about fifteen minutes before. The last of the skyscrapers was vanishing now through our sleeper car's one large window.

My stomach rumbled. "I was probably hungry hours ago. The adrenaline kept me from really feeling it until now."

Cable took his glasses off and stuck one earpiece against his lips as he looked out the window. It was only about 5:30, but being the winter solstice, it was the shortest day of the year. The sun had set a little while ago, the New York skyline twinkling at us like white Christmas lights before it vanished out of sight. "Riding a train is relaxing, isn't it? I rode a lot in Europe." His relaxation was all him now. I'd been sure to remove the enchantment I'd cast on him once we'd gotten settled, just so the fear and anxiety didn't hit him at the wrong time. Unlike me, he hadn't screamed or panicked or anything when my enchantment had been released, so maybe it had worn off before that and I just hadn't noticed.

Not everyone bottled up their fear to be discharged all at once at one wrong moment.

Still, I hadn't yet talked to him about the Grimms and the kids too observant for their own good. We'd only just settled, and Cable had been sorting through his research notes and I hadn't wanted to unload it all on him.

At least the train ride rather than the car ride home might give him more chances to collect his thoughts for his research paper.

He sat on the bench kitty-corner from me in our cramped roomette. This close, that musk that hung around the professor, like pine and old books, brought comfort and a sense of home to even the tiniest of spaces. The whole thing was a wonder in getting the most out of what room there was. The bench Cable was on turned into one small bed, then the other pulled out from the wall above the window. The small one-person seat I was on was cushioned and had an arm desk that I could pull out and retract back into the wall behind me beside a small sink.

It was also on top of a toilet.

There was a genuine toilet beneath the cushioned seat I was on if I flipped this and that around. Might have been nice for solo travelers, but Cable and I hadn't reached go-to-the-bathroom-in-your-chair-while-the-other-one-is-one-foot-away status quite yet. Thankfully, there were a couple of larger public bathrooms at the end of the car, complete with shower stalls.

"There's a dining car, of course." Cable set aside his scuffed, brown folio bag in which he kept all of his notes and research and stretched his arm behind him to grab a pamphlet stuck to the wall. The pamphlet seemed wrinkled and well pawed-through, but beside it was a crisp white piece of paper announcing the "Holiday Crossword Puzzle Event." The game was set to start at six o'clock in the dining car Cable had mentioned.

"We should get there in time for the crossword event," I said, reaching across Cable in the cramped space to show him the flyer. The tip of Broomie's shaft, the part I thought of as like a tail at times, hung out of the small luggage compartment above the pull-out upper bunk. We'd left it open when she'd decided that was a cozy enough place for her to ride along. Her shaft was swinging back and forth lazily like a contented cat's.

"We wouldn't be proper Games Club members if we didn't," Cable said. "Any good with crosswords?"

"No," I admitted, taking my comfortable toilet seat chair again. "You?"

"Well…" Cable put his glasses back on and scratched the back of his head. "I mean, I *am* an English department professor. Vocabulary, I've got down. But pop culture trivia? Not so much. I wonder what kind of crossword puzzles we'll need to do."

Hmm, so Cable had an advantage if it was more random-vocabulary themed, huh? I hoped that was the case. I was sure to be even less helpful when it came to pop culture trivia. I'd basically been living under a rock for almost thirty-one years. The rock growing on my arm in Luna Lane.

Still, I didn't care what Rhys Willywalla Snootnose said. We were going to at least *try* to give the man a run for his money. I wished Faine were here. She kept up with a lot of the cool things other people did, especially the stuff popular with kids.

"We should probably arrange our pickup." I winced. "And tell everyone about the car accident."

Cable frowned and rummaged through his folio, pulling out his smartphone. "My mom's going to freak out. She might try to drive and meet us halfway, though the train isn't even stopping before Chicago." He looked from me to the phone and back. "Maybe we can ask Faine to pick us up if she's able, like you suggested?"

I laughed and took the phone from him. I didn't have my own. Hadn't needed one before I'd left town. "She's going to find out at some point."

Cable took a pen out of his bag and slipped it behind his ear, staring at his notepad a little too closely. "Tomorrow," he mumbled. "After we're back."

"I'll tell Faine to keep it quiet." I stared at the phone, handling it like a master, if I did say so myself. Cable had let me borrow it whenever I'd wanted during the trip, and he'd programmed Faine's number into his contacts so I could catch her up on everything I'd been up to and vice versa. I clicked on her picture, seeing her bright, cheery bright-red-lipstick smile light up her pallid complexion in the image I'd had Cable take when he'd added her contact. She had her dark hair in soft curls around her face, as well as a bright red paisley headband that had matched her red vintage dress, which was cropped out of the frame.

"Hello?" Faine said when she picked up. "Dahlia, are you on your way home now?"

"Yes," I said, though my voice kind of squeaked. It wasn't a lie, but...

"What's all that noise?" Faine asked. Ironically, a clattering occurred behind her on her end. It was nearing time for her café, Hungry Like a Pup, to close up. They were more of a breakfast and lunch place, early dinner if you could swing it. Then they got some food ready for First Taste, the pub run by vampires next door, if you really needed some restaurant cooking after the werewolf family had gone home. Theirs was the only café in town.

"Falcon, stop annoying your sisters!" shouted Faine. But then she burst into giggles. "Dahlia, you have to see this." She sent a notification she wanted to face chat, so I accepted and got an inside view of the café from back home. It was dark there, too, the street behind the broad café windows hard to see, but the eclectic diner interior was all lit up. Half of the chairs were flipped up and over onto the tables so the kids could mop. Flora, the oldest child at seven, held the top of the mop with one hand, her other on her hip as she looked down at the shiny linoleum floor beneath her. Fauna, the middle child, was shrieking, a mop still in her hand, as Falcon, the toddler, was running around on all fours like the werewolf he was, a sponge taped to each hand and to the bottom of his feet.

"You're messing up what I already mopped!" shrieked Flora.

Fauna, backed into the corner against the window, spun around and growled beneath a line of red, shiny garland, the temporary painting of a snowman and giant snowflake looming above her. It *was* getting closer to the full moon, I supposed. Another reason why I'd hoped to be home this week, in case the werewolf parents needed my help reining in any of their wilder children's urges.

Fauna's two puffy brown pigtails atop her scalp resembled wolf ears more than ever as she got on all fours and kept growling at her brother.

"*Mo-om!*" shouted Flora, exasperated.

"Who taped sponges to your brother?" Faine demanded.

"Well…" Flora grew sheepish. "It was Fauna's idea! He's always crawling around this time of month. We thought he could make it easier to mop."

"If you try to take shortcuts, sometimes it just creates more work," said Faine in full *Mom* mode.

Flora groaned and stomped past the view of the camera.

Faine was out of sight, but I could still hear her. "Now take those off your brother—and all of you, finish mopping. Do it right. Then we can go home and make a pizza."

"Pizza!" all three said at once. Three nearly identical streaks of different heights rushed past the camera.

"Pepperoni!"

"Sausage!"

"Bacon!"

Yes, it was definitely nearing the night they'd shift to full wolves. Not a mention of vegetables anywhere in there.

"Honey, did you put in the order for—oh,

hello… Dahlia?" Grady popped into sight in front of the camera, and I realized Faine must have leaned her phone against a napkin dispenser at the diner counter.

Grady was tall and thin, his brown complexion several shades darker than his children's, but the shape of his face so similar to each of the kids'. They all had his brown, coiled hair, styled differently. Grady kept his close-cropped. One of his arms was scarred and pocked, a result of my subpar healing.

"Hi, Grady!" I said, trying not to dwell on the evidence of my failure. "How's it going?"

"Fine, just fine. You're missing all of the holiday decorations around town this year. Spindra went all out with this blue-and-silver web outside her store. Hey." He leaned closer to the phone. "Are you on a train?"

"A *train?*" Faine snatched up the phone so fast, the jittering image was about to make me sick. She peered into the camera, her eye growing larger like in a fishbowl. "Dahlia Poplar, are you on a *train?* Where's Cable? Did you two fight?"

I laughed and shifted the phone to show Cable scribbling notes. He grinned and looked up, then waved. "Dahlia couldn't make me angry if she tried," he said. "But she's too sweet to even try."

I flushed and turned the phone back to me. "Car trouble," I said simply.

"So you just abandoned his car?" she asked.

"Well… More like *major pileup on the George Washington bridge this afternoon and we almost slid off into the Hudson River* car trouble? His car was wrecked."

"Ohmygoodness!" Faine gasped and Grady let out a soft whistle. Faine's fingers danced over her phone and I realized she was probably looking up the news. I hoped Ingrid, Cable's mom, didn't keep up with such things. Though she probably would have called if she did.

Faine's hand flew to her mouth. "You're all right?"

"We are," I promised her. "No one was seriously injured at all. We were lucky."

"I don't know if I'd call it 'lucky,' but…" Faine shook her head softly. "Oh, Dahlia, I'm sorry your first trip ended in such a stressful experience."

"Stressful?" I chuckled, wincing at my own memory of the fear that had caught up with me later. "Compared to the trouble in Luna Lane the past few months, I'd say we got off easy. I'm just not sure about spending much time in a car again."

Cable murmured, "Ride" to me without looking up from his notes.

Right. I still had another car ride ahead of me.

"Well, it's been peaceful the past few weeks here," Faine said.

"Yeah, it was probably just me."

"Don't say that." Faine *tsked*. "You lived here almost thirty-one years without incident…"

"And when trouble did come to town, a lot of it

had to do with *my* family," I pointed out. I sighed, looking up at Broomie in the luggage hold, knowing she was snuggled up against my invisible pike.

"*Almost* thirty-one?" Cable perked up from his notes, putting his pen back over his ear.

Faine must have heard him. "She didn't tell you? It's her birthday on the first."

Cable's eyes widened. "No! Dahlia, how could you not tell me it's almost your birthday? And that your birthday is *New Year's Day*?"

My shoulders bunched up under all the scrutiny. "It's not a big deal."

"It *is* a big deal," said Faine. "And we're having a party at my house. Café's closed for the day."

"I'll be there," said Cable, nodding and sliding his notepad back into his bag.

All right, then. I reddened, unsure what else to say.

"Faine, do you mind not spreading the news about us taking the train back—and why—before we get there?" Cable asked, raising his voice to be heard over the soft, repetitive rhythm of the train sliding over the tracks.

"Hmm, okay, but why?" Faine asked.

"Mom gets worried easily." Cable slid his glasses up his nose and knocked his pen off his ear. He picked that up, too, and flung it back into his bag. "But we need a ride home from Union Station in Chicago." He pulled the tickets out of his bag again and looked them over. "We'll be there at two in the afternoon tomorrow."

We still had a long train ride ahead of us.

Faine murmured something to her husband and I saw him nodding partly off-camera.

"We can manage that," said Grady. "One of us will drive out there while the other takes the café and the kids."

"Thank you," I said. "I'm sorry to put you out."

"That's what friends are for." Faine pressed her cheek up against her husband's and the two of them smiled into the camera. "We can't wait to have you home."

Home. Yes. Where I longed to be. But Cable's days in Luna Lane were numbered...

"I can't wait to see you," I said. That was the truth. "In person," I added, inspecting the phone in my hand just a bit. Normie technology was a form of magic in and of itself. I didn't think I could project images of myself and Faine across the miles to speak to one another.

My stomach grumbled, and they must have heard it across all those miles because they both laughed.

"Pizza!" cried one of the girls.

"I miss your cooking, too," I told the Vadases. Both Faine and Grady were amazing chefs.

"Well, I don't imagine we'll have any pizza left-over to save for you for tomorrow," said Faine, looking down, probably at one of the kids.

"*Nooooooo!*" shouted Falcon, clearly horrified at the idea of leaving leftover pizza.

"That's okay," I assured him. "We're off to the dining car now. There's a—" Before I could explain about the crossword puzzle event, the kids started to howl. I'd chat with her about it all later. "We should probably get going!" I said, louder to be heard over the howling and the noise made by the train.

"Take care!" Faine shouted back. "Stay safe!"

Looking out the window of our sleeper car, I thought over her words as I ended the call. Cable was right. Traveling by train *was* relaxing. Even the loud noises of the train operating were kind of a steady background, hypnotic in my ear.

What could possibly keep us from "staying safe" now that we were off those icy roads?

Chapter Five

"**I** promise I'll ask about cornhusks, Broomie, but I don't think they'll have any." I kept my voice low, hushed, as the door leading to the hallway from our sleeper car was partway open. Cable had just gotten back from the public restroom and we were headed to the dining car.

Broomie stuck her brush head out from the luggage compartment and her bristles drooped. They rubbed together in a little scratchy moaning sound.

I'd brought some along on the trip, of course, but she'd poked her little naughty head into my bag and eaten them all in the first three days. She didn't *need* sustenance for her health, but how she loved devouring cornhusks, the favorite treat of all witches' broomsticks, so my mother had confirmed to me once. Mom's own broomstick, Broomhannah, had also dined on them with relish, but perhaps also with more poise than my spunky Broomie.

"They're out of season. And I don't imagine they shuck any corn they use on the train on site." I was pleading now, trying my best to set her up for disappointment, though my heart was clenching at the thought. Even though I knew *I* was not the one being unreasonable.

Broomie twisted so both her brush head and the tip of her shaft tail stuck out of the compartment, the shaft whap, whap, whapping like an irritated feline.

"Who are you talking to?"

A little black-haired head popped up from around Cable to peer inside our sleeper car.

I jumped outside of the room and shut the door behind me, whipping around to lock it. "My friend. On a phone," I said, passing the keycard over the spot beside the handle and handing it back over to Cable.

January Grimm stared up at us from between our torsos, practically forcing Cable against the window in the cramped, narrow hallway. I still needed to confer with Cable about how weird these kids were.

"January, don't just dawdle there. Proceed to the dining car." Odessa lingered behind us in the direction of Car 13, ushering August forward.

With a blast of air, the door to Car 13 opened

behind them, the three elderly traveling companions I'd met at the station heading our way.

"Is this the way to the dining car?" Mabel asked loudly as she edged past the Grimm family as quick as a flash to cut in front of us. She cradled her dictionary under one arm, obviously eager to participate in the crossword puzzle event.

"Yes," said Cable helpfully. He gently squeezed past her in order to take hold of the heavy door. "Car 10. We're headed there ourselves."

"I *told* you it was Car 10," said Sally brusquely over the roar of the noise from the open door. She stumbled as the train shifted beneath us and muttered something under her breath as she slapped a hand against our roomette door, gripping on to the handle for support. Then she straightened and barreled past us as Mabel had, not even thanking Cable for holding the door for her.

"I *know*," added Mabel as they stepped into the chilly space between cars. "I thought we *were* headed to Car 10."

"Car 1 is the engine and the engine is *that* way." Dora edged past me and used the leather wallet she'd clung to at the station to point in the direction we were all headed now. She stumbled, too, speaking so softly, I couldn't really hear her and clutching the handle of the roomette beside Cable's and mine. I took hold of her shoulders and helped her find her balance. She stiffened and glanced up at me with a look of horror, which soon melted into a smile, perhaps when she realized she was no longer in danger of falling. "Thank you, dear," she said to me sweetly before making her way to the next car, being sure to thank Cable for holding the door, too.

Then it was my turn to thank Cable and step over the perilous gap in the ground below us, a steel platform over which I knew the train cars were hooked together. The rush of cold, bitter air reminded me my warming enchantment had worn off. The short, narrow walkway was rickety as well, the old ladies having barely made it through without tumbling. I felt like I was on a ride.

"The caboose, where that nice porter brought our spare luggage, is Car 30," said Dora. "*That way.*" She pointed behind us. They were still arguing about this. I wondered how far they had gotten in the wrong direction before turning around.

"All right, all right," said Mabel. "No need to get all snippy at me." She held her dictionary to her breast, using the other hand to grab the handrail along the window side of the hallway. As it was in our car, a simple string of green garland was strung along the window, giving the place a little touch of festivity. We passed another set of sleeper roomettes in Car 11, three rooms instead of two like ours had, and without the public restroom like in Car 12. Perhaps we shared the one at the back end of ours with a row of sleeper cars.

At the end of the walk, the brightly lit dining car beckoned. A number of people were already situated at several of the tables.

"Come, children. You're making the poor man wait. Though with such *strong* arms, I bet he could hold that heavy door all day." Odessa fluffed her hair and smiled broadly at Cable, her lipstick cracking, as she ushered her children into Car 11. Ahead of me, the elderly ladies made it inside the dining car, but I hung back, waiting for Cable.

January narrowed her eyes on me and moved forward, spinning around to keep looking at me practically until she got to the other end of the car.

"Hi again," said Odessa to me as she and August squeezed past. I got a much tighter, grimmer smile than Cable had.

August ran forward to join his sister and they both stood at the entryway to the dining car. As Cable stepped up behind me and we made our way forward, Odessa reached over the children's heads to push on the door. It took a bit of force, but she managed before Cable could finish squeezing past me to go help. January used two fingers to point to both of her eyes, then directed one of those fingers toward me before turning on her heel and following her mom and brother into the next car.

"Did you *see* that?" I asked Cable, grabbing him by the arm.

Cable shivered from the blast of colder air. "What?"

"She did that 'I'm watching you' thing I've only ever seen in movies."

"Who?"

Okay, so he clearly wasn't as attuned to these kids' weirdness as I was. *He* was the one with all the travel experience. Maybe the kids weren't as odd as I'd thought.

The short trip between cars was as frigid and as rickety as the other trip had been. Perhaps even more so, the noise of the train operating somehow even louder in this corridor connection, the air colder.

"Welcome," said a woman almost the moment we'd stepped in. "Take a seat anywhere."

Their argument unabated, Dora, Sally, and Mabel were settling into the nearest empty table for four. Behind them, January had stopped beside a smaller two-seater table just beyond Bedwyr's own, leaning rather strangely sideways across the table to peer face-to-face at the man seated there. Rhys Willywalla Snootnose or whatever his name was. He glanced up briefly and held a hand over the left side of his collar, his lips mumbling something before the little girl, seemingly cowed, scurried away.

Cable directed me to another table with bench seats up against one of the windows, and I was about to follow him when I did a double take. The hostess who'd greeted us and was now serving Bedwyr at a two-seater smaller table near the car door was the woman with the "Lien" nametag who'd brushed past me on the escalator into Penn Station.

So she did work on a train. This train in particular.

"Cable." Bedwyr nodded at us as we passed. He took a sip from a steaming mug half full of coffee and bit into a half-eaten croissant. "Dahlia."

Cable murmured his greetings back and we scooched down the narrow walkway between the two rows of tables.

"Do you mind?" Rhys looked up at us from his table beside us, an open puzzle book in his left hand that had its cover bent entirely to wrap around the back, a fine-tipped, expensive-looking silver pen in his right. The shiny, silver cap was absent from his front pocket now, the black letter opener handle the only item left sticking out of his coat. Of course the man did puzzles in pen instead of pencil. On his table rested a steaming tea cup on a saucer full to the brim with what I guessed to be tea, a small white plate with brown crumbs all that was left of whatever small dinner he'd ordered. Even his crumbs were orderly, though, just a couple at the edges, almost as if they'd just crumbled whenever the chef or server had placed the item on there and not a single crumb had fallen from this uptight man's lips. He yanked his small folio bag away from where it rested practically in the walkway against his ankle.

"Pardon me," said Cable, moving on.

I glared at Rhys and didn't offer an apology.

Cable slid into our selected booth first, facing westward, and I took the other side, though I realized with a wince that it put the Grimm family—three booths down past a few more tables full of other people and another empty table—behind me. Cable wouldn't know to keep an eye on those kids.

Almost as soon as we sat down and Cable had grabbed a menu from where it rested behind the napkin dispenser, a little beeping sound went off and Bedwyr stood up, munching the last few bites of his croissant.

"Gentlepeople, please listen," he said, projecting his voice loud enough to be heard over the steady rhythm of the train. Lien headed down the walkway, offering me a small smile as she passed our table. "It's six o'clock, and that means the start of the Speedtracks Overnight Express Holiday Crossword Puzzle Event!"

Rather than being strung across the windows like in the sleeper car walkway, the dining car's garlands hung down from the ceiling, over the tables. Perhaps they didn't want to cover the fine red 'Do not open unless in event of emergency evacuation. Alarm will sound' lettering over the windows. There were cardboard cutouts of winter and holiday figures like Santa and his reindeer hanging from the front of a counter to my left, behind which was an array of bottled drinks. Lien settled in behind the counter, wiping it down with a white rag.

"Everyone who is participating, please raise your

hands! Don't be shy! This is an all-ages event, so everyone qualifies!"

Rhys's hand shot up, even as he continued to work on his own "warm-up" puzzle book, not bothering to look up. All three elderly ladies we'd walked in with also raised their hands, as did Cable and I. I looked over my shoulder to see pretty much everyone in the car except for Lien had raised their hands. And Odessa. Though her children both waved their hands in the air eagerly.

"Good, good. Exciting to see so many eager puzzle enthusiasts!" Bedwyr bent down and lifted up his briefcase, settling it on the table in front of him. His mug jostled and even from several yards away, I saw a drop of liquid fly out and hit the white cloth tabletop. Deftly moving the dials on one end of his lock, he opened the briefcase with both hands, as if the contents were worthy of some reverence.

He took out a book with a black-and-white crossword evident on the cover, along with a sheet of paper with a similar black-and-white pattern and a pencil. "Here are the rules. The event begins today, as soon as I pass these out to each participant, a collection of higher difficulty challenges and a brand new sheet with a puzzle tailormade for the event. These can only be completed *in* the dining car, where I or one of the train's staff"—he gestured to Lien, who was in the midst of taking a sip from a mug on the counter and wriggled the fingers on her free hand at all the heads turned her way—"will supervise. While participating in the event, I must ask that you leave your smartphones, tablets, laptop computers and any other aid there at the counter in that basket."

Murmuring broke out amid the group as Bedwyr turned to put down his demonstration aids and rifle through his briefcase. Though no one else seemed to be paying attention to her anymore, I watched as Lien put her mug down in front of a man at the counter. She fidgeted in place, scrunching her shoulders up and wincing as the man looked at her, puzzled, then picked up the mug and glanced inside it.

Lien quickly turned around to grab a clean mug and filled it with coffee before placing that mug in front of the man and taking away the other one, speaking to him softly all the while. He scratched his chin for a moment but chuckled, sipping from the new mug.

Had she mistaken his drink for her own? While on shift?

Bedwyr motioned for the room to calm down, swaying just slightly as the train glided into a curve. "Yes. So. We'll collect your aids now. I assure you we will keep a close eye on your belongings—or feel free to keep them locked away in your compartments before you make your way here. I can't let anyone have an advantage. This must be done entirely from the knowledge in your head."

"What about dictionaries?" asked Rhys, narrowing his eyes on the table of old ladies. His pen kept moving in his hand, reflecting the overhead lights as it moved so brightly, I practically had to shield my face rather than keep looking at him.

"Dictionaries are not permitted, either, of course." Bedwyr clutched the table with one hand as the train finished its curving path.

Mabel muttered something unintelligible and tossed her dictionary beside her with a loud whap that made me jump. She was seated alone across from Sally and Dora.

Rhys straightened in his seat, a smug little smile just barely upturning his mouth beneath his too-thin moustache.

"Madams, may I ask what this is?" Bedwyr gestured to the elderly ladies' table and picked up the handmade large, brown leather wallet held together by a bit of elastic around a button. The one Dora had clung on to at the station.

"A knitting needle case," Sally snapped, yanking it back from him. "Do you suppose we stuffed an entire dictionary into that, too?"

"No, I just thought it best to put all loose items in the basket I've arranged for collection. It'll be quite safe there, I assure you." He turned over his shoulder and addressed the waitress. "Lien, can you bring the basket?"

"*We* find it *best* you keep your hands off our property." Mabel narrowed her eyes, first at Bedwyr and then at Lien, who approached with the basket, as if *daring* either of them to take their stuff away.

"Uh, yes… Yes, of course." Bedwyr balked and waved Lien away from the three ladies, adjusting the tie at his neck, and went back to stand nearer his suitcase. "Just this once, then." He sent an apologetic look to Lien, who stood there beside him with the empty basket.

Lien made her rounds through the car, but we'd left Cable's phone in the roomette, so we had nothing to put in the basket. Rhys didn't add anything, either.

"A lot of knitters like to knit in restaurants," said Cable quietly to me. I *had* thought it odd they'd brought theirs with them, though I did think Bedwyr was being uptight by trying to confiscate it. "My mom does it, too. Though usually only when she's dining on her own."

"Now," said Bedwyr, drawing our attention once more. "These paper crossword puzzles are worth a total of two hundred points. That's five points for every correct word. You will be provided with the opportunity to complete a special event crossword once every four hours. Yes, I plan to be out here in the dining car overseeing the participants the entire train ride."

One of the kids let out an audible groan and Odessa hissed. "Hush now. You have a bedtime." So the kids weren't going to be puzzling all night.

Yawning and stretching my legs out across from

me on one side of Cable, I didn't think it would be worth it for me to forgo sleep, either.

Let Rhys stew in his sleep-deprived winnings. If he was as good as he claimed, maybe there really was no point in fighting the inevitable.

Still… It would be nice to pay Cable back a part of the travel costs.

"I know some of you will move faster than others, and this is where these books come in." Bedwyr lifted the book in the air again. "Standard fare, a wide variety of themes, with the answer keys removed from the back of the books, these will be worth fewer points—a total of just one per correct answer—but they shall tide you over until the release of the next special event puzzle. And if you complete a lot of them, the points will add up either way." Bedwyr tossed the book back into his briefcase and put his hands on his hips. "Any questions?"

Cable's hand shot up.

"Yes, Cable?" Bedwyr asked. He turned to the rest of the crowd watching. "Forgive me, yes, I'm aware I'm being so informal with him by addressing him by name, as I do all my colleagues. I know this gentleman—we worked together for a brief time—but I can assure you there's no creativity involved in judging this event. Only correct answers, not buttering up the judge, will get you far." He snickered at his own joke and drummed a hand across his slightly protruding belly.

"What do we do when we want to go back to

our compartments?" Cable asked once Bedwyr had finally quieted.

"Glad you asked! Turn in all of your work to me—you should write your names on both the book and the papers I hand out—and then when you return, I'll return yours so you can continue where you left off." He tapped the side of his nose. "Yes, I know this may give an advantage to anyone with a good memory who might rush out to look up those answers they just couldn't think of, but barring any silly business, like frequent back-and-forth jaunts, I think we should be all right." He gestured toward the western end of the car. "There's a restroom there, so if you feel the need, you can leave your work on your tables and head there. Just check out with me whenever you think you'll be gone from the dining car for more than a moment."

"Any more questions?" Bedwyr asked. He peered over my shoulder and I looked over to find August's hand shot up. "Yes, young man?"

"Can we work in teams?" he asked softly. Bedwyr didn't hear him and we had to pass the message down along the train.

Rhys bristled.

"No, sorry, young man, please conduct your puzzle solving in near total silence. You and your mother and sister there can each enter as well. Gives you three chances of winning."

"Oh, I'm not entering anything that involves letters up, down, and backward," said Odessa.

Backward… Backward… Like a witch's enchantment.

"There is no backward in crosswords, Mother," said January.

"Not unless it's a very advanced cruciverbalist at work," Rhys muttered, his nose still in his own puzzle book, but I could hear him.

"Anything else?" Bedwyr asked.

No one stirred.

"In that case, let the first annual Speedtracks Overnight Express Holiday Crossword Puzzle Event commence! Well, not actually quite yet. Please wait until all participants have the materials in front of them before you begin. Let me pass out the material. Lien, do you mind helping?"

The waitress walked back around the counter, leaving her rag behind, and approached Bedwyr's table, collecting the material he handed to her.

"Remember, phones, tablets, devices, please into the basket on the counter!" Bedwyr shouted over the murmurs of conversation. "Oh, and of course, dictionaries!" He clapped his hands toward the three elderly ladies.

"I'll *basket* you," said Mabel clearly, her eyes narrowed. Whatever that meant, her intentions were clear.

"Or to the side of you," said Bedwyr, taking a halting step back. Either his nerves or the movement of the train caused him to sway somewhat. "Just for this first round, mind you. Best to refrain from bringing them into the dining car whenever you plan to participate."

Lien approached our table, a stack of materials against one of her arms. "You're participating, correct?" she asked, that friendly smile on her face.

"Yes," Cable and I said at once. "And may we also put in a food order?" Cable asked.

"Careful," I said, arranging the pencil Lien had offered me in a neat stack next to the puzzle book and the first sheet of paper. "Bedwyr might think we've hidden some hints within the food."

Lien giggled beside us, and I felt myself blushing. I wasn't used to making strangers laugh.

"I'll be right back to take your order," she said, moving on to the table behind us. The hair sticks holding up her messy bun caught my eye as she passed. One was plain red and smooth, the other bumpier, more cherrywood in color. The top of just that one had a puff of brown fur.

"Now remember, please don't start—in fact, please turn those special event crossword puzzles over until we officially begin," said Bedwyr, making his way down the aisle with his own stack. He paused in front of Rhys, who was transfixed on the paper in front of him, his empty plate and full mug pushed across to the spot where no one would be joining him.

Bedwyr flipped it over, and Rhys looked up at him and growled—actually *growled* for a moment, his brows drawn together in a menacing glare—before stiffening and sitting straight up.

Bedwyr laughed nervously. "Surely, a champion of your ilk doesn't need the extra time to formulate his answers."

His face warping an almost unnatural shade of green, Rhys looked positively about to be *sick*. Rather than remark on anything, though, he picked his pen up and went to work on the puzzle book he'd brought with him, which was currently on his lap to make room for the event puzzle book and paper.

Cable turned around, focusing on Bedwyr instead of Rhys. "Champion?" he asked.

"Yes." Bedwyr beamed. "I learned about that just now. Mr. Aloveius told me he—"

"That's Mister *Wallaya* Aloveius, thank you," said Rhys, his pen a flurry.

Bedwyr's Adam's apple bobbed and he looked between Rhys and Cable with a strained smile on his face. "Yes, Mister… Wallaya Aloveius. Our paths have not yet crossed—it's a wide world out there, the champion crossword game, so that's not too surprising."

"Is it really?" Cable asked. "Such a wide world of contenders?" I didn't think he'd *intended* the question to be rude.

"Wide, yes, though not so wide a member of the so-called London Puzzle Society should be unclear on who the reigning champions currently are." Rhys sneered, still not looking up from the puzzle book on his lap.

"Well, I… I've only worked with the Puzzle Society for a short while," started Bedwyr.

Rhys actually looked up at that, his pen frozen in his hand. "*That* much is clear." His face turned that odd greenish shade again, and he snapped his attention back to the puzzle book on his lap.

The door far behind me to the next car opened with a loud gush and Bedwyr brightened, snapping his head in that direction. "Ah! Conductor Zapatero! How wonderful of you to join us."

I peered over my shoulder to see that perfectly poised conductor I'd seen on the train platform make his way down the dining car, his hands behind his back. "Glad to see so many participants in this event." He turned to Lien, who was at the counter now, putting down the last of the puzzle materials in her hands in front of a man who waved them away. The middle-aged man with a hunched posture was making short work of some soup. "Lien," the conductor said, "are you getting everyone's order?"

Ah, right. The Puzzle Society may have been sponsoring the event, but the train was probably only poised to make money by taking orders. Unless the contest had urged people to buy tickets, which I supposed in Rhys's case had to be true. But if his skills were to be believed and he walked away with refunded train fare, well, the train wouldn't have generated any extra money there.

"Right away, sir," said Lien. She looked sheepish, like she'd just realized she'd forgotten that part
of her job, though I knew that wasn't the case.

"And the roomette check?" he asked.

Lien looked around nervously and seemed to
notice me watching the exchange. I wasn't the only
one. "I'll get to it… sir," she said.

"See that you do." The conductor mumbled
something about "newbies" and moved forward into
the next car, the burst of air and the louder rhythm
of the train on the tracks hard to ignore.

"Right, then," said Bedwyr, nodding at us.
"You may flip over the special event puzzle and
begin. The first theme, of course, is winter
holidays."

Rhys, fastest to flip his paper over with a *thunk*,
snorted.

He didn't appear to have much holiday cheer.

We went to work.

"Hmm," said Cable after a couple of minutes of
virtual silence in the car—though I could hear Lien
softly taking orders several tables back. "I can never
remember all of the reindeer's names."

A pencil came down with a whap against our
table, startling us both. "No conferring about the
clues, please." Bedwyr's jaw was set despite his
customer-service smile.

Cable rubbed the back of his head and I sent
him an apologetic look. Only once we'd both gone
back to focusing on our papers did Bedwyr walk

away. I hadn't felt this tense at a table with a pencil in my hand since my last high school exam.

I hadn't gone to college for obvious reasons, though Cable had mentioned online courses during this trip. I only had the library computer as far as internet connection went. Or maybe Sherriff Roan's computer at the station. But he needed that for work, and it was awfully slow.

I wondered, with better internet, if Cable could teach in Scotland remotely…

Lien reached our table and took our order and by the time I turned in my completed special event puzzle—Rhys had infuriatingly turned his in at least twenty minutes before and was working through his bonus puzzle book with gusto—Cable gave up and turned in his, too, despite the empty spots remaining.

"Are you *sure?*" Bedwyr asked Cable, taking the papers from us as Lien brought over our dinners. My stomach rumbled at the aroma of ratatouille and steaming hot French bread for dipping. Bedwyr barely moved aside to give Lien room to do her job. "You have another three hours before the next puzzle is released, you know. Plenty of time to think it over."

Cable winced, but his face brightened as Lien set a baked cod dinner in front of him, complete with diced potatoes and coleslaw. "I'll be asleep then. Dahlia and I have had a long day." He looked to me for confirmation and I nodded. Maybe in the morning, I could make up for lost time with the puzzles I'd have slept through.

Bedwyr frowned but walked away, shuffling the papers he'd collected as he approached his table with his open briefcase.

As I enjoyed my meal, I looked around, taking in the rest of the dining car. Almost everyone had moved on to eating, though I noticed Dora, Sally, and Mabel were all working on their bonus puzzle books with one hand as they ate with the other. Either all ambidextrous or that determined to beat Rhys. Rhys himself was working on the puzzle book, at least several pages folded over already, and I had to imagine he hadn't skipped any, rats, and he refused Lien's offer to warm his tea. She'd offered to refill it at first, but apparently, the man was so focused, he still hadn't drunk any.

Our meals were cleaned away and Cable and I both had a decaf coffee and a scone for dessert. Cable was giving the bonus puzzles a try but frowning, often staring out the window behind me. I was halfway through the first puzzle in the bonus book myself when I thought we should get back to our roomette, not least of which to check on Broomie. My chest felt tight with a thought that I'd promised to at least *ask* for cornhusks. I wondered if there was something similar—lettuce?—I might be able to transform into cornhusks, but no. There was no fooling Broomie's refined taste buds.

"Lien," I asked as she passed by with some of

the elderly ladies' dishes stacked over her arm. She brightened when I'd called her by name. "This probably sounds weird, but do you serve... corn?"

She arched a brow. "We have a rotating menu, but I'm sure there's corn back there somewhere. I can ask. Do you want some to take back to your roomette?"

"No," I said quickly. Cable snickered even as he didn't look up from writing a word down in his puzzle book. "I was just wondering if... you have any cornhusks. In your garbage."

Lien blinked. And blinked again. She tilted her head and seemed almost to be pointing one of her shoulders behind her. "You mean, like, for crafting...?"

"Yes!" I said, eager for the save. A few tables behind Cable, Dora looked over at us. I kept my voice quieter. "Please. If you don't mind asking."

"Sure," said Lien, though her smile seemed strained. Or pained, even.

Maybe my ridiculous request was just the last straw of a challenging customer service day.

Cable hummed "Jingle Bells" quietly as Lien walked away. Dora went back to working on her puzzle book. I did, too.

Beside us, Rhys slapped his pen on the table—hard. "Will you cease that infernal sound you call a melody? Please?" Despite the use of "please," he wasn't asking politely *at all*.

Cable's eyes widened behind his glasses, as if he

hadn't realized he'd been the one humming. I shot to my feet, slamming my pencil down on my open puzzle book. "There's nothing in the rules that says we can't even hum!" I started. "If a *champion* can't focus because of a little noise..." I gestured out toward the window, my gaze darting that way as the train rounded another corner, the cars at the back clearly visible as they were dragged around the bend. "On a *train* of all places, which is hardly the quietest—"

I gulped, having lost my train of thought.

On the very last car, just barely visible in the flash of a lamppost amidst the dark of the night, was a person. On top of the train.

Chapter Six

"There's a man!" I shouted. Or at least I thought it was. The silhouette was on the bigger side, anyway. "On top of the train!"

But just as everyone's heads turned to peer out the side of the train where I was pointing, the caboose rounded the corner and there was nothing for them to see.

Rhys, who hadn't so much as leaned an inch to get a better look, kept up the quick movement of his pen over paper. "The depths to which you'll go to interrupt this contest."

I spun on him. "This is *not* some ploy to make you do worse on a *crossword puzzle* contest!"

"Now, now," said Bedwyr, lowering both hands in front of him as if to calm the hysterical woman. Me. "Surely, it was an innocent trick of the lamplight. Now please take a seat, Miss Pope, or I'll have to ask you to finish your dessert and leave this car to those actively participating."

The ladies behind Cable bristled and murmured amongst themselves as Cable squirmed in the booth. "Maybe we *should* just go," he said. "I should probably get some more work done on my research paper before we turn in."

"It was *not* a trick of the light." I turned around, taking in everyone's bewildered—or in Rhys's case, bemused—expressions. Everyone except… "Where's Odessa?"

The Grimm twins were seated at their table without their chaperone.

A toilet flush rang out across the relative quiet and then there was the sound of running water. No one stirred for a moment more until Odessa stepped out from the single stall in the dining car. Wiping her hands on her skirt as she took the few steps down the walkway to her table, she jolted a little under the stares of most of the car's inhabitants. January flashed me an impish grin and sat up straight in her chair, her hands folded together atop her open puzzle book as she slipped to the side to allow her mother back in the booth.

"What did I miss?" Odessa asked.

"Nothing—" started Bedwyr.

"A poor example of sportsmanship," snapped Rhys.

So Odessa hadn't been the figure on the caboose.

But… if she *were* a witch, particularly one of Eithne's caliber, couldn't a teleportation enchantment to and from a single-person bathroom go unnoticed?

I barely even registered Lien approaching from Car 9, where I imagined the kitchen to be, based on how frequently she'd traveled back and forth. She held up a doggy bag and stopped in front of me. "Chef told me I was welcome to them. I just had to… dig through… the compost." She sighed.

I cocked my head.

"That… *material* you asked for?" I spotted a thin line of corn silk dangling from the fur on her hair stick at the back of her head. She *had* done some digging for it.

"Oh! Thank you." My neck growing hot, I took the bag from her and finally sat back down. "I appreciate it." I knew one broomstick who would bristle-kiss the poor woman for it if I'd allow her to show herself in public.

Broomie! Maybe she'd seen something. We couldn't communicate in words, exactly, but she had her ways to answer my questions when I needed her to.

The door to Car 11 burst open and Conductor Zapatero came barreling through. I'd never seen the man losing his composure. Not even when everyone had been scrambling to board the train.

"Hello, Conductor Zapatero—" started Bedwyr, but he let out a little wobbly cry as the super-serious conductor pushed past him, speaking into a walkie-talkie on his shoulder.

"Engine, confirm status," he said, sending the crowd gathered in the dining car into a tizzy. He didn't seem to notice the effect his words had on his passengers.

"All clear," said a static voice in reply. "Did you confirm the source of the—"

But the conductor had reached the door to Car 9 and yanked it open, the rest of the reply drowned out in the whoosh of air and the steady chug, chug of the train on the tracks before the door slammed shut again.

"Well, if *that* doesn't inspire confidence," Dora said. "Ladies? Shall we retire to our rooms?"

They had multiple roomettes? Well, it did seem like each sleeper roomette could hold two passengers max.

"Please drop off your puzzle books here," said Bedwyr, his voice a bit shaky at the conductor's strange brief appearance, but he straightened his bowtie and leaned a hand on the table beside his briefcase. "Come back after you've rested—the next event puzzle drop is at ten o'clock."

"Too late for my blood," said Sally as she stood, grabbing Dora's needle case.

Mabel clutched her dictionary book to her chest and practically tossed her puzzle book at Bedwyr, who fumbled it but managed to catch it before it hit the floor. "Some of us have some studying to do before next round." She tapped her dictionary against her temple.

Rhys let out a *harumph* sound. He was back to work in his bonus puzzle book.

"But, *Mother*, we have to come back at ten o'clock," whined January as her mother led her family of three down the walkway and back toward Car 11. "We have to do all the event puzzles or we won't win!"

Rhys *harrumphed* again, punctuating the sound with something like a small cackle, but no one but me seemed to notice.

"In the morning, dear." Odessa directed the twins to drop off their puzzle books at Bedwyr's briefcase. "They can make up for the puzzles they missed overnight in the morning, right?" Her voice had a chirpy quality, almost hopeful.

"Yes, yes, of course, children. Don't you worry about it. The event isn't over until 1:30 tomorrow, half an hour before we pull into our destination."

Grumbling, the twins accepted their fate and followed their mother into Car 11, Sally, Mabel, and Dora getting up from their booths and heading in that direction shortly behind them.

Was I letting my imagination run wild again? Would a wicked witch out for my secretly-royal blood *care* about the results of a crossword puzzle event?

All that amateur sleuthing I'd been doing back home was getting to me.

Whatever I'd seen on top of the caboose, the conductor was clearly aware there was an issue.

My teleportation skills were still untrustworthy, especially on a moving target. What was I supposed to do? Take Broomie for a flight above the train and check it out for myself?

Blinking, I gathered up my doggy bag, pencil, and puzzle book, and stood up.

"Ready?" Cable asked.

"Yes," I told him, grabbing his puzzle book and dropping both of ours off at Bedwyr's briefcase. I was eager to get back to our car so I could let Cable know about my idea.

Cable took a few more moments to catch up, arranging payment with Lien—I was so used to living off tabs and paying every once in a while en masse in Luna Lane that I'd almost forgotten—but I waited for him just inside Car 11.

The doors to the three sleeper roomettes in this car were all wide open, Mabel's voice carrying out from one of them.

"They wouldn't *dare*."

"I told you," said Dora saccharinely sweet. "I told you not to bring your valuables with you. Why you must *always* travel with your favorite, I should hardly know. Told you we wouldn't need it, but—"

"'You never know when you might need one,'" Sally added loudly, almost as if shouting, clearly mocking someone.

"Well," said Dora. "Won't do a lot of good out of our possession."

Someone let out a roar. "What were *you* doing?" Mabel shrieked, and there was that sound again, probably of her dictionary hitting something hard. Like a table. Or a rock.

The door to Car 12 burst open and Odessa came back in, practically stumbling on her heels as she shrieked and shrieked and shrieked.

The door behind me opened at the same time and Cable stepped through, the sudden vortex of having both doors open at once enough to send me stumbling, my cheek hitting flat against the cold window beside me. The top of my head jostled some of the garland dangling from above.

"What's wrong?" Cable asked.

From the three open roomettes, out popped a series of heads. The roomette nearest the panting, sobbing Odessa housed Mabel and Dora.

The roomette west of that contained Sally and a giant ogre of a man. I realized with a start I'd labeled him a "pallbearer" in my head when I'd seen him and two others solemnly carrying an inhumanly large trunk down to the platform.

From the roomette closest to Cable and me, there was another one of those men.

Getting a better look at their faces—square jaws, sharp eyebrows, bulbous noses, even the grayish tone to their wan, peach skin—I realized they could easily be brothers.

The third man they'd been with was nowhere to be found.

Cable asked if I was all right, helping me back away from the window. When I replied that I was, he ran down to Odessa, who was clutching the handrail along the walkway behind her. "What's wrong?" he asked again and she leaned forward into him, seizing both of his sharply defined biceps.

This woman was so often in distress, part of me wondered if it was all to make *my* knight in shining armor swoop in to save her.

Was it an act?

"It's… It's been taken!" she shrieked. Then she started sobbing, burrowing her brow against my boyfriend's chest.

If this wasn't an intentional act to unnerve me, she had some explaining to do.

"What has?" Cable asked. His hand hovered over her back, squeezed into a fist, then flexed outward again, settling for three gentle taps at the top of her shoulder.

"It's *gone!*" she moaned, not elaborating.

"You, too?" Mabel asked. She readjusted her glasses.

That got my attention. I spared a quick look at the nearest pallbearer—he looked at me blankly, like he didn't get what was going on. Neither did I, really. "Was something taken from your rooms?" I asked as I made my way closer to the commotion.

"Yes." Sally crossed her arms tightly across her

chest. Her eye darted quickly to the pallbearer beside her. Between them, I spotted something open on Sally's bench seat. A purple velvet trunk, the lock of which seemed busted.

What was this man doing in her roomette with her?

Sally seemed to notice my curiosity and shot me a dazzling smile. "I was just asking our sleeping car neighbor here if anything was stolen from *their* room, too."

I turned to the man with her. He also stared blankly, blinking almost inhumanly slowly.

"Was something taken from you, too?" I asked.

He shook his head, back and forth, not saying a word.

"We should tell the staff," said Cable, speaking louder with each syllable to be heard over the woman wailing in his arms.

"Could it have to do with that man on the caboose?" I asked those around me.

They all stared at me—even Cable—as if I were as dumb as a rock.

No comment on the fact that there was gargoyle blood in my veins.

"I *wasn't* imagining it!" I shouted, glaring at Cable in particular.

He shirked back, then I stared pointedly at the woman in his arms and he shirked back some more.

"Here," he said to her, gently bringing Odessa

outward to arms' length. "Why don't you sit down? Where are your children?"

Odessa produced a dainty violet handkerchief she'd been clutching in her spindly hand and dabbed her eye. "In our room," she said. "Searching to see if anything else is missing."

Cable nudged her toward Dora and Mabel's roomette and the two women exchanged a glance and a silent conversation, probably to wonder if they wanted this wailing drama queen in their compartment, but they stepped aside and let Cable usher her inside. The small space looked just like our own, and he directed Odessa to the bench seat that converted into a lower bunk. I hovered outside in the walkway, Mabel and Dora backing up beside me to allow Cable space to maneuver Odessa inside.

"Perhaps we should get the conductor," Cable said, stepping back. Odessa let out a particularly high-pitched wail and when she couldn't reach for Cable any longer, she threw herself over the bench as if it were a fainting couch and started sobbing into her arms. Her fingers brushed against Mabel's dictionary on the bench, splayed open, revealing a fairly ornate design for a simple dictionary.

The inside of the cover was golden in color, even shiny in the overhead light, and I caught a flash of red before Odessa shoved it aside and the book fell closed, revealing it had been covering a rather large rock.

Gray, slightly bumpy and oval-shaped. Just a regular old rock about the size of a musk melon.

What was that doing there?

"I don't know if we need to make a fuss as to all of that," said Dora sweetly, smiling broadly up at Cable as he awkwardly shimmied past her to stand beside me.

"But you said something was stolen from you, too—" I started.

Then my heart just about burst out of my chest.

Broomie!

Leaving the wailing chaos and gathering crowd behind, I flung open the door to Car 12. Barely holding my balance as I traversed the rickety area between cars, I yanked open the next door and found two sleeper compartments with doors wide open.

Which included ours in the middle between the other, apparently empty, roomette and the bathrooms.

And in front of that door were the bottom halves of the Grimm twins as they peered inside my roomette.

Chapter Seven

"Ohat are you doing?" I charged up beside the Grimm twins, hovering over them and fighting the urge to grab them by the backs of their clothes like a mama cat and her kittens' scruffs.

"Nothing," said August, leaning back and flattening himself against the handrail at the edge of the walkway. He trembled, his large eyes even wider as he stared up at me.

"Investigating," said January simply. She tilted her chin as she straightened up, as if to challenge me to find fault in what she'd said.

"Investigating what?" I demanded to know.

I peered up at the luggage compartment. We'd left it open to begin with, but there was no sign of Broomie's brush or shaft dangling over. Good because I didn't want the kids to have noticed her. Bad because I was terrified whoever had rummaged through everyone's compartments and stolen things had taken my precious broomstick.

I charged past January and reached up into the luggage compartment, feeling around. There was Cable's luggage, my bag... Something long and hard.

Broomie? My heart soared.

I felt again. No, this was too cold, too smooth.

My onyx pike turned invisible. So the thief had totally missed that. Not that I'd expected otherwise. It was invisible and entirely too large to easily abscond with even if it hadn't been.

But Broomie? Could the thief have realized her value? What if she'd come to life in front of them...? What if they'd fought or Broomie had even chased the person onto the roof?

What if...?

"Broo——" I started, swallowing when I realized the kids were watching me.

Beside me, the cushion seat covering the in-roomette toilet jostled, lifting up just a bit. A shaky, small clump of bristles popped out, curling up into an angle like a thumbs-up sign.

Letting out a sigh of relief, I tossed the doggy bag onto the bench seat and sat down.

"Dahlia?" Cable hovered in the doorway beside January. August was barely visible behind them. "Is Broo... Is everything here?"

"Yes," I said, relief flooding my voice. I shifted, looking to the side of me and noticing Cable's folio.

"That is, I think. I didn't open any of the luggage yet." I handed it to him and he stepped inside, flipping it open and rummaging around.

"The only thing I have of value for a thief is my phone." He pulled it out of his bag to show me, then dropped it back inside, ruffling papers. "Everything else seems to be here, too."

Good. It'd be awful if he'd lost any of his research after all the effort he'd put into it over the last few weeks.

January and August peered back into the roomette around Cable.

Why were they still hanging around here, with their mother distraught the next car over? *Investigating*? What did they suspect me of?

Almost as if on cue, the toilet seat cushion lifted just a *little* higher, enough to allow one long tendril of bristles to knock over the doggy bag beside me on the bench with a crinkling crash.

January tried pushing forward more, and I leaped to my feet in the cramped space to block her view entirely as Broomie, still mostly hidden beneath the toilet seat, managed to unfurl the bag and pull the cornhusks out and under the toilet cushion with her. The cushion cover cluttered back into place with a loud *clonk*.

Even under the cushion, and despite the cover of the steady rhythm of the train over the tracks beneath us, there was the chewing, too, as Broomhilde worked the husks through her bristles and they absorbed into her magically. Broomsticks —even enchanted ones—weren't equipped for digestion.

January tried to push past Cable, but he was rather large. He just clasped his folio and leaned over to place it next to me, seemingly oblivious to the whole thing. January narrowed her eyes on me. "What's 'Broo'?"

"Don't you have to go be with your mother?" I snapped.

I was snapping. At a child.

Cable swirled to face the children, his hands hovering behind their backs as if to direct them outward. "We have to go alert the conductor. Your mother said something was stolen?"

January's nose wrinkled as she allowed herself to turn the corner. "Yes. Something very precious to her."

"Precious to her," August concluded. They sounded as if they were reciting a line she'd fed them or were otherwise just overly bored of the affair.

The door opened and that whooshing rush of air slammed Cable and the kids flat against the handrails on the opposite side of the doorway.

I peered out into the hallway as the door banged shut and Conductor Zapatero entered from Car 11. "Anything taken from this car?" he asked brusquely.

Cable shook his head. "Not from our room."

"I'm going to have to ask everyone to return to

their rooms for the next hour," he said. The door behind him opened again and Odessa hobbled in, the force of the chill air and her distraught state making it more of a challenge than it ought to have been. "Come on, children. This nice man is going to find out what happened."

Cable frowned at the conductor as Odessa ushered her children away toward Car 13. "There's a thief on board." It wasn't a question.

Conductor Zapatero tilted his hat at Cable. "That is why I'm asking everyone to please return to their seats or rooms. We'll make an announcement overhead when you're free to walk around once more."

"What about the bathroom?" whined August from down the walkway.

"We have one in our room," said Odessa, her voice still trembling.

"Gross," said January.

"You can head to the bathroom, but that's it," said Conductor Zapatero. "Now please. Back to your seats. I've radioed ahead to the police. We haven't made any stops, so if there's one thing I'm sure of—the thief is still on this train."

Unless I'd spotted the thief in action *on top* of the train.

Cable yawned, not looking up from his work as he scribbled away on the bench seat kitty-corner from me.

Until our evenings in hotel rooms, I hadn't spent much time around him working. I could stare at him all day and watch the furrow of his brow, the way his mouth opened just slightly when he seemed about to launch into a rapid pace of writing, as if an idea had struck him.

He almost seemed to forget I was even here.

Broomie stretched from her position on my lap where we sat on the cushioned toilet seat. There wasn't any water in the toilet—it ran on pressure, I assumed—but I'd cast a "NAELC" enchantment over her just the same when I'd let her out.

Broomie nudged her head against the paper doggy bag, but it was empty. She knew that because she'd checked it three times since devouring its contents already.

"Cable, I want to investigate," I said.

My introverted professor finished scratching out whatever sentence he was working on without looking up. "Investigate what?"

"The thefts, of course."

Cable put his pen down. "Dahlia, that's a matter for the professionals."

"Maybe ordinarily," I said. Broomie gave up rummaging around the empty bag and stretched as much as she could, shaking the very tips of her bristles in separated clumps like little toes. "But I bet most train thefts don't involve a culprit on the roof."

Cable winced and grabbed my hand. "Sorry I seemed like I doubted you. It just sounded so…"

"Weird?" I offered. Broomie was lazily flying in circles above our heads, getting frustrated with bristly grunts every time she ran into a wall in the compact space. "Unnatural?" I tilted my chin upward at my flying, living broomstick.

Cable nodded thoughtfully. "You don't think…?"

"That Broomie and I are not the only paranormal presences on board? Yes, I do think that." I couldn't say anything with definitive proof, but things weren't adding up—about the Grimms, the figure on the caboose roof, all those presumably locked sleeper roomette doors left open, the missing items…

"Did Odessa or the old ladies ever tell you what had been stolen from them?" I asked.

Cable shook his head. "I don't think they were calm enough to talk about it." Well, that was true for Odessa, but not so much for Sally, Mabel, and Dora, surely? "Besides, I'm sure they explained it all to the conductor."

Broomie settled up on the open luggage compartment, disappearing inside entirely.

"What if they didn't want to say?" I ventured. "What if the things… weren't easily explainable to a train full of normies?"

"Like what?" Cable put an elbow on his knee and leaned forward, giving me his whole attention. Above him, Broomie seemed to be rummaging around in the compartment, a scraping sound like a rock being pushed across a solid floor centimeter by centimeter hard to ignore.

"A potion?" I ventured. "Some enchanted item?"

"A witch?" Cable's voice was hushed, as if the idea of a witch on the train haunted him, as if she could pounce on him if she heard her kind named.

I sent him a bemused look.

"You don't think Odessa Grimm is… odd?" I asked.

Cable wriggled his eyebrows. "I don't like to judge people."

I nudged his knee with my own. "Sure, Mr. Aspiring Investigative Journalist." It was a joke between us. The usually honest, amiable professor had managed to fool me for days.

"My bad," he said, rubbing the back of his head. Above him, the scraping noise grew louder and stopped suddenly, Broomie poking her brush head back out. "What is it, girl?" Cable turned to look up at her above his head. He stood but with a *clonk* sat back down again, his jaw open and his eyes squinting as he rubbed the top of his scalp.

Standing, I reached above him, next to Broomie's head. Sure enough. My hand hit cold, smooth metal. She'd pushed the onyx pike partway out of the compartment.

"Broomie, you want me to take this?" I asked. She nodded her brush head eagerly, a bottom clump of bristles lolling downward like a tongue in an eager puppy's open mouth. Carefully, I took hold of the invisible spear and tried pulling it, but it kept clonking on the opposite wall. "NIAGA ELBISIV," I said, and the shiny black onyx came back into view. It was a little easier—though still difficult—to wrangle the pike out of the compartment now that I could prevent it from slamming into the tightly packed walls. It was weighty, so I strained to hold it above my head. How had Cable gotten this up here in the first place?

One end fell with a loud *clunk* to the ground as I finally managed to remove it from the compartment entirely.

"She probably wants you to have that if you're going to fight a witch," suggested Cable.

Broomie bounced eagerly, slipping out from the compartment and curling up on his lap. She'd been good about not scaring him on this trip as she'd promised. He pet her brush absentmindedly, and for a moment, my heart melted at the sight of the two of them getting along at last. Cable had been afraid of Broomhilde since we'd been children.

I stared at the tall pike. It was heavier these days in my hand. I switched it to my left—my arm that had handled it so well a month ago. But that was when I'd had an arm full of stone scales, and I supposed it'd been my gargoyle blood inside of me that had made it easier to hold.

This pike had belonged to my father, I'd learned. My gargoyle father.

Though why a stone golem brought to life to protect a witch princess would have wielded a weapon capable of ending a witch, I didn't yet know. I needed to ask Eithne.

If I could bring myself to summon her spirit from the realm beyond upon my return to Luna Lane.

My muscles strained as I tried to lift the weapon. "I don't know if I can handle this without my stone scales," I said. So there'd been no point in bringing it with us. Not that I'd expected to ever need to remove it from Cable's car, except in case of emergency.

Cable frowned and took hold of part of the pike's shaft. "Can you make it smaller? Lighter?"

"I don't want to mess with it," I said. "Especially without the right potions, without… speaking with my aunt." I spoke that part quieter. He knew why I would have been hesitant to summon my aunt's spirit before we'd left. My feelings toward her were complicated at best.

If I'd talked to her, though, perhaps I also could have transformed it into a playing card for easy traveling.

"Well," said Cable, taking the pike from me and

sliding it into the small gap between the toilet-cushion and the bench beside it so it leaned vertically against the wall, "it's only really useful against witches, right? Let's hope it doesn't come to that."

"Yeah," I said, but my voice was lackluster.

What had I intended to do? Stomp over to the Grimms' roomette and run through the mother of two young children with it?

No. Not even if I had proof she was a witch. Not unless she gave me no choice.

Broomie let out a little chirrupy groan as her head watched the pike. Surely, she wasn't so blood-thirsty as to be disappointed I wasn't planning on using it, right?

She'd had a wooden staff herself, which she'd wielded against Broomholly, Eithne's broom, when the pair had given us little choice but to fight back. We'd left that behind somewhere in the lake. A broom would fall if her witch did. There seemed to be little reason to attack a broom first. Wherever a witch may have been hiding one aboard this train.

"Well, so far, you just have a hunch, mostly," said Cable, picking up his notepad again.

"Thank you for your patience, passengers," came Conductor Zapatero's voice over the loud-speakers. "We are currently conducting an investigation into the theft of several items in passengers' compartments. Authorities have been alerted and have given us permission to allow passage throughout the cars. Please make your way to the dining car if looking to eat or participate in the special crossword puzzle event, and feel free to take showers if you have sleeper car tickets. Otherwise, we do ask that you remain in your rooms as much as possible until we're all clear." The loudspeaker crackled with static.

"They don't know who the thief is yet?" Cable asked.

"Yet they're letting the crossword puzzle event go on..." I snatched Cable's smartphone up from on top of his folio bag and checked the time. Ten o' clock. There'd be another new event puzzle.

"I'm headed back," I said, setting the phone on top of his bag.

Cable frowned. "To investigate?"

"Maybe." I shrugged. I wasn't entirely clueless at this type of thing. "But I wanted to solve more puzzles, too." I hoped that would allay any fears he had about me heading out just now. "The dining car is bound to have plenty of other people there. I doubt anything untoward will unfold before my eyes."

"Well..." Cable scratched his cheek. "I think I'm out of the game. I already messed up that holiday puzzle." Suddenly stopping himself, he picked up his phone and typed quickly across the screen. "Dasher! Vixen. I always forget those two." He set his phone back down and gestured across the bench. His notepad and several books lay scattered. I knew he'd been checking his phone for research and images he'd taken on the trip as well. "And I really feel like I'm making headway here."

"It's fine. I can represent Games Club for the both of us."

Cable chewed on the tip of his pen. "I *am* a failure as a member of Spooky Games Club, aren't I?"

"Well, this game isn't *spooky*," I pointed out. So far, pretty much every type of game we'd tried out as a club had managed to end in some paranormal disaster. "So you're good."

Cable smiled back at me, then nodded to Broomie, who'd settled sullenly on his lap, her "tail" end of her shaft swinging lazily. "Take Broomie with you. I'd feel better."

Broomie perked up, her brush head swirling at Cable, then to me.

"All right," I said. What was the worst that could happen? If anyone who didn't know the significance of my "walking stick" noticed, they'd just think I was eccentric. And Odessa had told her children they couldn't come back to the dining car for the ten o'clock puzzle. But if they did—if either acted weird about my broomstick—maybe that was the tell I'd been looking for that they were really a family of witches.

Chapter Eight

Despite the late hour, almost as soon as I shut the door to our roomette, January and August Grimm wandered up to me from the direction of the bathrooms. Since I knew their roomette was in Car 13, their presence here confirmed that a number of sleeper cars shared the same bathing facilities.

They were wearing matching gray-and-black flannel pajama sets, their feet in fuzzy black slippers.

Each draped a towel over the same arm, their dark hair even darker when damp.

"Why are you holding a broom?" January asked, her little button nose turned up in the air.

Bananaberries.

Broomie was stiff in my hand, but I started making a sweeping motion across the narrow walkway floor. "I thought it was dirty out here."

August pointed up at Broomie's brush, which

hovered at about shoulder-height. I was so used to carrying her this way. "Most people brush with that end."

"Most train *passengers* don't go brushing train hallways at all," added January. Her lids grew heavy as she zeroed in on me. "Least of all with an ancient, raggedy old broom like that."

Broomie bristled, shaking her head just slightly, letting out a chirrup sound. I laughed nervously to cover her distress before flipping Broomie around quickly and dragging her bristles across the floor. "Silly me."

"Broo…" said January thoughtfully.

My back straightening, I turned on my heel and headed toward Car 11 without another word.

It wasn't until I was at the second door between cars that I realized I had two children tailing me.

Once we were all inside the car, I spun on them. "What are you doing? Your room is the other way."

January thrust her chest out, the towel over one arm making her look like a fine dining waitress. "Our mother is asleep."

"She was so very distressed," added August.

"And…?" I asked, waiting for them to elaborate.

"And we are going to solve our ten o' clock puzzle," said January, all matter-of-fact.

I frowned. Part of me didn't want them around, just in case they were normies. They'd seen too many things. But if they weren't… And how *could* they be normal?

"I don't think your mother would approve," I said.

"I don't care," said January, challenging me to disagree.

I was about to engage in a stare down with a kid twenty years my junior when the door behind August leading back to Car 12 opened up, Rhys Snootnose barreling through.

"Out of my way!" he shouted, pushing—literally *pushing* the Grimm boy aside.

"Hey!" I cried.

He glowered at me as he shimmied past and I shot him a matching look back. He faced forward almost immediately, giving me a good look at that scar of his I'd noticed. It trailed up from under his collar and around the back of his right ear.

January and August seemed unperturbed, using my distraction to push me aside and head to the dining car.

So be it. I'd be able to keep a better eye on them.

Once the door to Car 11 slammed shut behind me, Lien stepped up from around the counter. At the table nearest the door, Bedwyr was sorting through his briefcase to produce the puzzle books for Rhys and the children. He started by handing each of the kids a sheet of paper with the new event puzzle, then dug through his briefcase to find their books. So *he* had no qualms about letting the children stay here unsupervised past their bedtime.

"I was here first," Rhys said, positively seething. "I'll thank you to hand me my puzzles." Despite Bedwyr's protests, Rhys practically knocked Bedwyr aside and took hold of the judge's briefcase with both hands, rifling through the items contained therein.

"Now, see here, sir, you can't—"

But Rhys wasn't finished, seemingly unable to find what he was looking for as he kept digging and digging and digging. The children exchanged a silent glance and headed down the walkway toward the booths as Bedwyr moved in to try to nudge the man aside.

"Ah! Here we are." Rhys practically slapped the shorter man across the top of his shiny bald head as he drew out his puzzle book with a flourish. He snatched a sheet of paper out from the briefcase, too, then took a seat at the same table as before, his back to the entrance to Car 11 this time.

"*Well.*" Bedwyr started sorting through the mess of papers all across his table.

"Miss?" Lien drew my attention back to her, going so far as to lean forward to block my view of Bedwyr so that I snapped out of what I realized was an intense stare. I wondered how long she'd been trying to get my attention.

She looked at Broomie in my hand for an obvious moment but didn't say anything. "Anything I can get you? If you want anything brought to your roomette, I'm also in charge of hospitality for the sleeper cars between here and Car 15." She brushed a lock of black hair that had escaped from her bun behind her ear. She looked like she'd had a long day. "I'd have introduced myself earlier, but I've had my hands full in the dining car."

"Oh, thank you. I'm mostly just here for the puzzle." Looking around at the largely empty dining car and realizing no one had been allowed in it for the past few hours, her statement struck me as odd. Then again, I didn't know anything about what her job entailed. She nodded and retreated back down the walkway to speak with Rhys.

The pompous crossword champion waved Lien away without a word.

It was my turn to accept the puzzle from Bedwyr's outstretched hand, though he wasn't fully paying attention as he organized his briefcase. His gaze went flat, his mouth falling open just a little as he turned around. Almost like he hadn't expected to see *me* at all. "Is, uh… Is Cable coming?"

I shook my head. "Research."

"Ah." Bedwyr's eyes darted to Broomie. Oh. Right. Maybe that was why he had a shocked expression. He cleared his throat and looked pointedly away, almost as if doing his best not to stare. Perhaps he thought me eccentric. "Always his nose in a book, that one."

Well, not *always*. There'd been plenty of activity that had gotten his attention in Luna Lane.

Smiling politely at him, I wandered to the

nearest open booth. I'd sit here, observe the children until they got tired enough to go to bed, then make my excuses to wander around a bit down the rest of the cars. The conductor had asked us to limit our activities, so if it came down to it, I'd find a quiet passage between cars and exit out the emergency door so Broomie and I could do a little of our own investigation outside of the moving train. "Maybe coffee?" I said to Lien as she made her way back down the walkway. She stopped and stared at Bedwyr, but he still had his back to her. "Caffeinated?" I added, to which Lien raised an eyebrow but didn't comment on it.

I did plan to sleep eventually if my investigation turned up nothing, but after everything I'd been through today, I could use the boost.

"Sure thing," said Lien, suddenly all business again. "And your husband?"

My eyes fluttered rapidly. Then I blushed. "Oh, he's my… um, boyfriend. And he's working back in the roomette." I wondered if he could use the caffeine boost or if it would be better if he slept. "Perhaps you could bring him some chamomile tea whenever you get the chance? Car 12, Room 2."

"Will do." Lien turned on her heel and stopped by the kids' table, the booth in the middle of the row that Cable and I had occupied earlier.

"Kids, anything for you?" Lien asked. "Did your mother tell you you could be here?" At least someone else was concerned.

"Mind your business," said January flatly, picking up her pencil and going to work on the new event crossword.

"Blueberry muffins," said August, copying his sister's movements as he also went to work. "Two."

Lien shot me a look like she couldn't believe those two, but my attention was drawn back to Bedwyr, who appeared at my tableside.

"The second event puzzle's theme is *mystery*," he said, pushing his glasses up his nose. "By which I do not mean the theme itself is a mystery, but that the clues refer to all things mysterious." He laughed at his own joke. "Kind of like the mystery we have on our hands in this very train, wouldn't you say?"

I chuckled awkwardly. "Was anything of yours taken?"

"No." Bedwyr turned around and patted his briefcase. "Everything I need is in here. I didn't bother booking a roomette since I'll be up all night at my post here, observing the crossword puzzle event."

"What were you doing when the conductor had us all locked down?" I asked, wondering if he'd seen anything of note.

Rhys sighed at the table beside us, but I sent him a glare in the barely discernable reflection in the window beside him. Outside, the countryside was dark, full of endless plains broken up every few minutes by clusters of trees.

"Oh, I stayed here, scoring crosswords. If you

flip through your puzzle book, you'll find I've tabulated your points already. Doing some late-night cleaning?" Bedwyr asked, pointing to Broomie. I'd leaned her on the booth beside me without thinking much about it.

"It's a walking stick," I muttered sheepishly as I took hold of her again. "Sometimes I'm a bit unsteady without her."

Bedwyr tilted his head. *Bananaberries.* Who referred to their walking sticks as "her"?

"Well, I was going to say it was a fine specimen. Fine, fine specimen—they don't make brooms like that anymore."

Broomie shivered in my hand just slightly, and I knew she was trying to stop herself from stretching out or dancing with pride. Laughing nervously, I patted her shaft to remind her to hold it in.

"How'd I do on the event puzzle?" I asked, bringing his focus back to the puzzles he seemed keen about.

"Oh, perfect score. Perfect score. You, that little Miss Grimm, and Mr. Wallaya Aloveius are the only ones who managed that so far." Bedwyr turned to his briefcase and started straightening the remaining books and papers. There were quite a few yet without participants here to pick them up and I wondered if the fun of the event had worn off for other passengers or the news about the thefts had kept most people in their seats or roomettes. There was the late hour to consider, too. Hmm. If I put my mind to it, maybe I'd have a chance of sending Rhys home with the black mark of failure.

"The event puzzles only get more difficult from here on out, though," said Bedwyr, and as he moved to close the lid of his briefcase—again with two hands and utter reverence—I swore I saw the very top of it shifting, drooping down at an unnatural angle, a shiny red color reflecting the fluorescent light overhead before he shut it closed and turned the lock.

"Did you bring any devices?" Bedwyr asked, putting his hands behind his back. "Anything you need to check in?"

"No," I said. "Just my walking stick."

"I wonder if your *walking stick* has any space between those bristles to hide a note or two," said Rhys. He didn't look up, his event puzzle just about finished in front of him.

Only when I opened my mouth to say something to him did he look up and glower, slapping his completed event puzzle over on the table before opening the event bonus puzzle book.

As if I were going to cheat off him!

"Here's your coffee," Lien said, standing in the aisle beside me. The kids both had muffins on plates in front of them, and August was picking off pieces with one hand as he worked on his puzzle with the other.

"Thank you," I said, arranging my crossword materials in front of me before taking a sip.

It was bold and made me shudder, but it might have been what I needed if I couldn't cast an energy enchantment on myself with all of these witnesses. I could always enchant myself to be sleepy later when I was ready for bed.

The coffee sure beat the taste of an energy potion, though. Not a single potion I'd ever brewed had tasted good.

The car settled down into near silence, the four of us still competing at work while Bedwyr sat back down and worked on grading Rhys's completed puzzle, I presumed, as it was now missing from in front of the champion. Bedwyr looked and caught me watching him. He smiled awkwardly, almost painfully, and I felt guilty for having stared, so I quickly turned back to my puzzle.

After a while, Lien stopped at my table again. "Anything else I can get you?" In one hand, she carried a doggy bag and in the other, she held a Styrofoam cup I thought might hold Cable's tea I'd asked for. She'd written "Car 12, Room 2" on it, so it had to be for him.

"No, thanks," I said, wondering how she'd planned on getting me anything with her hands full anyway.

Lien pursed her lips a little and looked over her shoulder at Bedwyr and Rhys. "I'll be back shortly," she added, louder to be heard over the clinking of the train. "I need to *confer* with my *colleague*."

"We'll watch the fort for you." Bedwyr chuckled. "Unless…?"

"Oh, no, *locomotor* business, not event business," said Lien quickly. Had she mispronounced *locomotive*? Did people still call trains that? Odd, but what did I know about what people called anything outside of Luna Lane? "Mr. Hamdi, please just *watch the fort*. Miss, I'll be back."

"Yeah, sure," I said, barely realizing she was talking to me now because her conversation was distracting me when I was trying to concentrate on the puzzle. I needed to think of the seven-letter name for the detective who always said, "Just one more thing."

A slurping sound made me do a double take and I watched Lien as she took a sip from the cup in her hand. Her focus was entirely on the men behind her, Rhys hard at work on his puzzle and Bedwyr rummaging around in his briefcase. Was that cup *not* for Cable, then? But why else had she written my room number on it…?

I was about to ask, though I wasn't even sure how to or if it was any of my business, when Broomie turned her brush head just a little as she spotted the doggy bag, which I was *positive* didn't hold any cornhusks, but I couldn't exactly tell her that.

Across from me and over the back of August's head, January glared at me, then looked at Broomie, but my broomstick had gone perfectly still.

Surely, one could assume she could have rolled a bit due to the movement of the train.

The room to Car 11 opened up, the loud thunder of the train rolling over the tracks diverting my attention. Lien was gone before I could ask if the drink was supposed to be her own or if she'd sipped on it without thinking.

What kind of server drank things for customers without thinking, though? Then again, I'd seen her do it before, with that man's coffee.

Weird.

Bedwyr caught me staring after her, even after the door shut, and he tapped a finger over his lips as if studying me and *thinking*. Thinking about what, I couldn't be sure. Probably wondering if I was somehow cheating.

I turned back to my event puzzle. On top, I'd written "Dahlia Poplar" without putting much thought into it. Cursing my carelessness, I erased my last name and wrote "Pope." I hoped I hadn't done that the first time, though Bedwyr hadn't mentioned it. Despite the heaviness in my gut, I still wasn't sure why I didn't want people outside of Luna Lane to know. As if I'd run into someone who'd met one of my relations.

But better safe than sorry.

Rhys snickered at the sound of my eraser on paper, and I knew he assumed I'd messed a word up.

Now I wanted to win this thing more than ever.

Minutes passed, and I couldn't shake the feeling that Bedwyr—or someone—was still looking at me, so I tried not to give them anything else strange to consider. Though there were still several words I was missing, I felt stuck. I decided to open the puzzle book to give me a break—maybe the event puzzle answers would come to me later—when the door to Car 9 burst open in a loud whoosh of air and Conductor Zapatero ran through the car.

Actually, *ran* through.

"Conductor?" asked Bedwyr curiously from his table, but the man didn't even get so much as a second look as Zapatero opened the door to Car 11 and rushed through.

Bedwyr and I stared at one another, and I looked around at the rest of the dining car. January and August were also peering after the conductor curiously, though of course Rhys hadn't bothered to so much as lift his pen off the paper for more than the time it took to write one letter and move on to the next.

"I'll go make sure everything's all right," I said, grabbing Broomie and sliding out of my booth.

Bedwyr stood as I passed him. "Oh, checking out for the evening already? Should I collect your crossword puzzle materials?"

"Sure," I said, waving a hand dismissively at him. That wasn't my main focus right now.

"But if you plan to come back, you're more than

welcome to leave your things here." He nodded toward Broomie, and I hugged her closer.

There was something a little strange about his furtive glances toward her. My gut told me not to linger. Maybe he'd seen her moving and wanted to verify.

"No, thank you. I'm done for now." I brushed him off and passed through the corridor to the next car on unsteady feet. I didn't have to go long to discover the conductor's destination.

"I absolutely *refuse* to accept this!" said Mabel. "You cannot keep us from wandering the train! We need our exercise."

Conductor Zapatero hovered in the open door to her roomette. "It's a safety issue, ma'am. If you have a roomette and are not in need of the restroom or the dining car, we ask that you remain inside it."

I could hear Mabel's scoff from here. "I suppose you think we'll be *safe* in our rooms? The rooms from which our treasured items were stolen? Our *locked* rooms, I might add?"

"My staff told me you were headed toward the observation car," said the conductor.

"Yes!" cried Mabel. "To observe! That *is* what one does in an observation car, is it not?"

"We know for *a fact* other passengers have been there," added Sally.

"Not all of the other passengers have roomettes," said the conductor, clearly exasperated.

"It's Speedtracks' policy. In the event of an emergency, we must enforce—"

"You're lucky we *let* you," muttered Sally, though she was overshadowed by Mabel's louder shriek.

"And I suppose running this train non-stop when there have been thefts on board is *Speedtracks' policy*, too?"

I approached the conductor now and he spared me a glance, his eyes doing a double take over the broomstick in my hand, but he didn't say anything to me. People were surprisingly polite about it. Most people. Without a child's lack of filter. "Ma'am, the authorities will be there to greet us upon arrival at Union Station. No one will deboard until they've conducted their investigation."

"And we're going to be *kept here* like criminals for hours while they do that?" That was Sally. As I peered into their room, I found her and Mabel in the doorway, their brows furrowed and a vein about to pop on Mabel's forehead, Dora calmly knitting what may have been a scarf on the bench seat behind them. "We're the *victims* here!" shouted Sally.

Mabel, holding her dictionary, flicked it open, rummaging through its pages. "I have just the thing for you."

Sally leaned forward to lay a hand over the book in the other woman's hands. "What good is that now? *Here*? With your favorite stolen?"

"I'm bookmarking a page for later!" cried Mabel. She bent the top corner of a page and slammed the book shut, only just missing Sally's fingers, and chewed on her lip, practically bouncing on her feet.

Dora's eye flicked to me before going back to focus on her work. "Now, now, ladies. Perhaps it's best we do as we're told. No need to cause any trouble and put on a show for all of these wandering eyes." Was she referring to me? Her knitting needles moved so quickly, it looked like they were joined together, the heads at the top so large and feather-like as to almost seem intrusive.

Conductor Zapatero opened his mouth, just as the door to the roomette beside the ladies' opened and out poked the head of one of those giant pallbearers, who stared at us—at me, at Broomie—with what could only be called curiosity. As if *I* were the cause of this ruckus.

But it wasn't that that stopped the conductor from saying whatever he'd been about to say.

A wind-tunnel-like sound echoed out in the air, the train car suddenly rocking, flinging us all sideways. I gripped on to Broomie with one hand and clutched the handrail behind me with the other.

Some kind of alarm then went off, the walkie talkie on the conductor's shoulder crackling with static.

"Conductor." The voice may have been Bill's

from up in the engine car. "Emergency alarm set off."

"I can hear that," snapped the conductor, speaking into his shoulder. "Which car?"

"Dining car. Car 10."

The conductor made to pick up his feet to run past me, but I moved quicker, running past the curious pallbearer—he was alone in his roomette, I noticed—to the doors leading to the dining car.

"Wait!" shouted the conductor. "Let me through!"

"NEPO!" I said to the handle, my voice drowned out by the loudness of the train's operations from the entryway. The door pushed back on its own.

Inside the dining car, the children were screaming, both of them. Bedwyr was over where the kids had been working on their puzzles, his knee on the booth seat, his arms stretched out and gripping—a leg. A small leg in gray-and-black plaid, which he held by the ankle.

"Help us!" he shouted over the sound of rushing wind. Two towels had flown into the air and were suctioned against the window. August launched at Bedwyr, grasping him by the waist and pulling backward, but he had little strength.

Rhys, meanwhile, was sitting where he'd been when I'd left, his reflective pen working its way over the puzzle book, his hat off his head and pressed against the counter across from him, likely kept there by the wind. His hair blew in the wild air and his left hand pushed down on the puzzle book to keep it in place—but he just *sat* there and kept working on it.

No matter right now.

"Slow speed!" the conductor shouted behind me, and his walkie talkie crackled.

"I'm trying, Conductor, there's—"

But I didn't wait to see what there was.

Someone had ignored that 'Do not open' sign on the window at the kids' booth, and now January Grimm was dangling out of the window, half in, half out, screaming but doing so with a smile on her face.

These weird, weird kids.

"Move aside," I ordered Bedwyr and August as the conductor trailed up behind us.

"But—" started Bedwyr.

I jumped onto the empty side of the booth, standing up on it, and stuck Broomie's shaft end out the window beside January. "Grab her!" I shouted.

"What?" she shouted back.

"EIMOORB BARG!" I shouted.

January did as I'd enchanted her to do.

"Go, girl," I shouted, and Broomie shot forward, fighting against the pressure of the wind, taking off like a shot so that January slipped back inside, over Bedwyr's and August's heads, and straight over the counter. She rumbled and rolled to a stop, Broomie clutched to her chest, atop the counter.

"WODNIW TUHS!" I flung both my hands toward the window, the wind drowning out my voice. I hoped.

The window slammed shut and the dining room went quiet, but for the steady chug of the train's movements, the last blare of the alarm, and the ragged breaths of everyone around us.

Everyone but Crossword Champion Rhys.

Chapter Nine

"Ah." An audible sigh escaped Rhys's lips as he leaned back in his chair.

As if *he* had just done a whole lot of work.

What was *wrong* with this man?

Frankly, there were too many things to list, but this wasn't *normal* eccentric.

Did that mean he wasn't *normie*…?

Rhys got up, snatched his hat back from where it had fallen on the floor after the window had shut, and affixed it atop his head before sitting down. Then he leaned forward and turned the page of his puzzle book, steadying himself before he began, his focus second to none.

That feeling he'd expressed, like some kind of relief had washed over him when he'd finished the puzzle before that.

I *knew* that feeling. It was almost like… Almost like he was cursed.

"Crisis averted." Conductor Zapatero spoke into his walkie talkie. "Medical needed in dining car."

Right. January. And even Bedwyr and August, in case they'd been injured in their attempts to save her.

Wondering about curses and crossword champions could wait.

"Engine? Report," said Conductor Zapatero.

He was met with static on the other end.

"Everyone, don't move in case of injury," he said, acknowledging those of us in the room. He straightened his hat and headed toward Car 9.

I guessed he hadn't noticed my enchantments, after all. And maybe he'd chalked Broomie flying to some kind of effect of the wind.

Medical… After the car accident, Cable had convinced me to not heal anyone but ourselves since the injuries had been relatively minor.

Looking around me, at everyone breathing hard, at January laughing—*laughing*—on her back atop the counter, there didn't seem to be too much to worry about.

Nonetheless…

"LAEH," I said as quietly as I could, directing my arms just slightly at January, August, and Bedwyr in turn, the word repeated softly under my breath. I didn't think any of them noticed me. But Bedwyr stared at me, his brow furrowed, chewing his bottom lip. I wasn't sure if he was actually hurt.

Thankfully, January shot up once the enchantment had taken effect, drawing Bedwyr's attention. She cuddled Broomie like a ragdoll, perhaps not even noticing how limber the broomstick was, bending at the girl's lap without issue.

"What did you say?" the girl asked.

Shaking my head, I made my way down the walkway and motioned for her to give me my companion broomstick. "Nothing. Now give her here, please."

January twisted and yanked Broomie away out of my grasp. "*She* saved me. And you did something. Several somethings." Her eyes narrowed.

She'd noticed my pronoun use with my broomstick. Massaging my temple, I closed my eyes for a moment. I could hear Broomie squirming slightly, her bristles moving, though I was sure she was still trying to stay incognito as best she could. "What even happened, January?"

"*Nothing*," January echoed snidely.

Bedwyr laughed, a bit strained. "I would not call that nothing, young lady." He looked around, as if realizing something for the first time. "Where is your mother?"

August sunk into the booth sheepishly. "Our room. Sleeping. She took some potion for better sleep."

"Potion?" I asked, swirling on him.

January rolled her eyes and started petting Broomie's brush head. "That's just what she tells him so he isn't horrified by our mother drinking wine before bed."

Or was *she* just lying because I'd shown my hand by reacting that way to the idea of a witch using potion? There *was* a sleeping potion that could knock you out so you'd appear dead. Eithne had used it to trick us at the euchre tournament in Luna Lane.

"Let me go get her. What car is she in?" Bedwyr asked.

I could have reminded him the conductor had asked us to stay put, but I knew everyone no longer needed medical attention. "Car 13," I answered for them. "Room…?"

"Two," August admitted.

January hissed at him like a cat. Broomie looked up just slightly, then turned her brush head toward me, as if to ask if this child were okay.

No, she most definitely was not.

"I should check on her. The children… The children need to be back in their room. If Lien returns, Miss Pop-Miss Pope, please tell her I'll be back to *watch the fort* shortly." Bedwyr brushed past me, offering me a flittering smile and a noticeable gulp, and opened the door leading to Car 11.

Pop-Pope? Had I written my real family name on the first event puzzle after all? But then why keep pretending to know me by the fake name?

And now that he'd brought it up, where *was* Lien? She'd left a while ago. Perhaps she'd gone on break? But no other staff member had come to the dining car to replace her.

Rhys let out a grunt once the door slammed shut behind him, slamming his pen down on the table in front of him. His leg bounced as he gazed out the window, at the dark prairie on either side of us.

"Can't do the competition puzzles without the judge to observe," he said aloud, as if speaking to the window. He rummaged through the folio bag he'd brought with him and pulled out... No surprise. A crossword puzzle book.

His eyes met mine as he opened his own book up, as if challenging me to say something. "The girl released the emergency latch," he said. "She was giggling the whole time and she stuck her head right out the window. Whether the rest of her tumbling out was intentional or not, I cannot say." He picked up his pen and went back to work.

So it hadn't been some paranormal occurrence, some dastardly deed? "January?" I asked, spinning on her.

She *harrumphed* and turned away, still hugging my broomstick.

I turned to her brother. He was easier to get to squeal.

"*Tell* me what happened." My head throbbing, I realized I was interrogating these two children like suspects.

"She said you would come rescue her!" He

ducked down beneath the table, though his head and shoulders were still visible.

"That *I* would?" I spun on January.

"LEAH!" she said, gesturing with her arms. It wasn't "heal" backward, but it was close enough. She'd heard me. "LEAH!"

Broomie took the opportunity to squirm out of January's grip and onto the tabletop. I snatched her up before January could, but she just missed her chance by a fraction of a second.

"That was dangerous!" I said. "You don't know *how* dangerous! And you're going to be in big trouble when your mother finds out what you did."

January sneered and crossed her arms. She was still seated, her legs out in front of her on the countertop. "Mother won't wake up until morning," she insisted. "And by then, she'll be all like, 'Groan! Leave Mommy be. I have a headache.'" January placed her forearm against her forehead and imitated her mom in a scratchy, strange-sounding voice.

Unless her mother was actually a demon of kind, it was entirely inaccurate. I shuddered. Were demons real? I'd never heard mention of anyone meeting one and one hadn't traveled to Luna Lane, but—

The door to Car 11 shot open, and we all turned—except Rhys, of course. I expected Bedwyr back with Odessa, perhaps, but I was relieved to see Cable headed my way.

I jumped forward into his arms, giving him a great big hug and a quick peck on the lips.

"Ew," said January, at the same time her brother said, "Aw."

Broomie bristled at being squished between us and I backed up.

Cable's ears reddened. "I guess you're okay?"

"I am, though we've had a *bit* of an adventure." I stared over my shoulder to glare at the kids. Only August seemed at all remorseful.

My gaze fell back on Rhys, still at work on his puzzle, and I frowned.

I had a lot to catch Cable up on, but I wasn't going to be able to do any of it with eager ears around us.

"Did you get the tea I had Lien bring you?" I asked, trying to direct the conversation to something that was safe. "She mentioned meeting someone to discuss train business, but she was carrying a cup for our room. I thought she might have dropped it off on the way."

Rhys slammed his book shut, then, as if our conversation were bothering him. The window being open and a child falling out, no, that wasn't a distraction. But me asking Cable about Lien, that was. The snob started packing up, standing and sliding his puzzle book back into his bag.

Cable didn't reply at first, also watching Rhys pack up. When the pompous man groaned and clutched a hand to his shoulder, his face growing pinched, it was hard not to stare, despite the glower he sent our way.

Flustered, Cable turned back to me. "Oh, uh, no. I, uh, I heard the alarm and ran around the train looking for you. I went the wrong way first, I guess." He lowered his face to whisper in my ear. "I thought you might be investigating the caboose, where you saw that person."

So he *had* expected me to be out here investigating. But so far, I hadn't done *any* of that.

Still, Lien had headed down toward the sleeper cars to meet with her co-workers a while before the alarm had gone off... And she hadn't returned since, despite the chaos. She'd forgotten the delivery for Cable entirely. Or she'd never had the chance to drop off that cup she'd been carrying.

Something didn't add up.

"Excuse me," said Rhys, though he didn't sound as if begging for us to excuse him at all. "Some of us have places to be." He exited out the door, the noise of the open air between cars earsplitting as he slipped through.

Did he, though? Wasn't he here just for this crossword event?

My thoughts were interrupted as the door to Car 9 opened behind us, the whoosh of air heralding the arrival of a middle-aged woman in a train uniform. She had on a white armband adorned with a red cross.

"Who got hurt?" she asked. She looked tired, her frizzy, auburn hair falling out of her bun.

"The children," I said before they could object. I'd let her stay with them until their mom arrived. Grabbing Cable by the arm, I turned him around and directed him to Car 11.

"Her, too!" said January. "Make her stay!" But she was drowned out by the whoosh of air and the thunder of the train wheels, followed by what reminded me of a pounding hammer echoing out along the metal, as we made our way into Car 11.

Rhys was nowhere in sight, despite leaving just a few moments before. Two of the sleeper roomettes were open as we entered, and ahead of us at the end of the car, someone quickly turned the corner from the direction of Car 12, where the bathrooms were, and entered the elderly ladies' roomette. I blinked, but I'd barely gotten a look. It had seemed to be an awfully tall person. One of the pallbearers? I glanced to the first open room to find two of the large men playing a game of cards in silence. The middle roomette, the one Sally had been using when whatever had been stolen had been taken from her, was still closed.

I peered inside the last room to find Dora and Mabel sitting on the bench seat, knitting a much longer scarf than I'd seen Dora working on before. It trailed between them over a thick book I could only presume to be Mabel's dictionary, black corners of the book jutting outward from beneath the knitted fabric.

"Everything all right in here, ladies?" Cable asked, peering over my shoulder.

I couldn't help myself. I stepped inside. Where had that monster of a man gone to?

I found only Sally in there with them, sitting on the cushion cover to their toilet, working on her own end of the knitting. Her needles, like Dora's, drew the eye—or rather, one did. One was a plain, unadorned piece of light wood, the other a dark brown with a clump of pine needles at the top.

"As all right as it's going to be, I suppose," muttered Sally. She yanked on the yarn connecting her portion of the knitted scarf to Dora's. It snagged on that large rock they'd kept with them. I'd have to ask if it was a souvenir of someplace they'd been on their travels or something. It seemed pointless to take such a large thing with you in a cramped space otherwise.

"Did someone else come in here?" I asked.

Mabel peered up at me through her glasses. Her eyes looked huge—bulbous brown—through the thick lenses. "Who? Sally? She has the next room, but we wanted to do some work together before going to bed." She'd paused in her knitting, and she seemed to have one half of Sally's plain pale cedar needle set. But her other didn't match Sally's more decorative one. It was white, uneven, riddled with black dots and tapering into a little tuft of black.

Sally was tall, sure, but hardly as wide as one of those men. But I clearly didn't see him anywhere before me. Before I could tell them what I'd thought I'd seen, Dora spoke. "I see you found her, dear." That must have been addressed to Cable. "What was that alarm about?"

Cable looked to me. I hadn't really explained anything to him, either.

"Accident in the dining car," I said. "No one was hurt," I added quickly. I gently pushed on Cable to direct him back to our roomette.

"Shame," said Dora behind us.

Shame there'd been an accident, indeed. She didn't know the half of it.

A half a minute later, we were in Car 12 and in front of our own room. I took hold of the handle. The door jammed. "It's stuck," I explained.

Cable frowned. "I didn't lock it. I was too worried about finding you."

"I don't think it's locked…" The door was moving just slightly, a gap evident. "It's just *broken*."

"Hmm." Cable looked around. "We can ask someone."

I waved a hand in front of the door. "XIF." The door slid open easily.

"Or that," said Cable, chuckling. "Sometimes I forget." We both stepped inside and Cable shut the door.

"Those kids are *strange*," I started, launching into an explanation of events. When I finished, I plopped down on the bench seat beside Cable's notes, books, and folio bag. Broomie stretched and shifted her little bristles into something like a yawn before settling down in a circle upon my lap.

"Wow," said Cable, sitting on the cushion seat above the toilet. "But it doesn't sound like anything paranormal was afoot."

Afoot? That had been one of the solutions in the second event crossword Cable had missed. He probably would have done better with that one.

"About *that*, though… I think Rhys might be cursed."

"Cursed?" Cable's eyes widened. "Are you sure?"

"I lived a curse every day for over thirty years. I recognize the signs."

"But you weren't actually cursed, remember? The enchantment kept you confined to Luna Lane to hide you away. The rest was your own blood."

Staring at the flesh on my left wrist, I rubbed my arm beneath my shawl. "Still," I said. "It was like a curse. The magic in my blood compelled me to do things, the sense of relief I felt when finished for the day—"

"And this Rhys fellow is what, cursed to do crosswords?" He snickered, but his smile fell fast when he saw my expression. "You mean exactly that, don't you? But more than one a day?"

"Not all curses follow the same pattern," I explained. *Bananaberries.* Another reason it would do me good to have an experienced witch I could summon around, but there was no space on this train to draw a rune circle and summon Eithne. Even if things *had* been pressing. Besides, I wasn't sure I knew the right runes by heart.

"Why is he here, then?" Cable asked. "Can't he just do crossword puzzles at home? Or does it have to be part of an event?"

I thought about it. I might have suggested the event being compulsory, but he *had* pulled out his own puzzle book for "fun" after Bedwyr had walked out and was no longer observing the fairness of the event. That wasn't the only time I'd seen him doing crossword puzzles on the side. It was like a compulsion with him.

Though I'd also seen him walk around *without* his nose in a crossword puzzle book a couple of times, too.

"I don't know," I admitted.

But something wasn't right here. What did I know for a fact? There was a thief, a likely curse, and a possible witch on this train… Other than myself, of course.

We sat in silence a short while, mulling it all over, when Cable's phone rang. I rummaged through his bag to hand it over to him when my breath hitched at the name displayed.

There was no image—though he could have appeared in one had he wanted to, whatever myths about vampires might have said—just a black circle.

"It's Draven," I said, slowly handing the phone toward Cable.

Cable held both hands up in surrender. "Faine put his contact in there. He's never called me before. I assume it's *you* he wants to talk to.

So Cable wasn't entirely oblivious to my ex-boyfriend's restrained hostilities toward him?

We'd hardly given the undead man a chance to contemplate the fact that Cable's true love kiss had broken the curse of my gargoyle blood.

It had been easier to just wish him a happy December and pack up and head on our way.

Easier for me, at least. I'd thought the time away would give him enough time to adjust to the idea before we had any meaningful conversations about it.

Maybe he would just pretend it wasn't of much significance to him and we could go back to the uneasy friendship we'd hammered out over the past few months. We hadn't dated in ages, after all.

Well, I supposed those years had gone by much faster for someone who'd been living half a millennia.

With a sigh, I dragged the green phone symbol into the middle of the phone to accept the call.

"Draven?" I asked.

"Why did you not tell me?" he snapped, his Transylvanian accent thick and on full display.

I exchanged a look with Cable, the phone on speaker between us in my hand.

"Tell you what?" I asked. Okay, I hadn't *actually* told Draven about the "true love kiss" thing—it had happened during the day, so he'd been asleep in his coffin—but I'd thought maybe town gossip would take care of that for me.

"That your motor vehicle slipped on the ice and nearly sent you careening off a bridge!" he shouted, exasperated.

Well, that was a relief. Sort of.

Come to think of it, I hadn't known he'd had a phone. I'd never had one, so I hadn't needed to get his number. Perhaps it was a relatively recent addition during those years I'd avoided him after our breakup, and he was still unused to using it. He was speaking far louder than necessary. I scrambled to turn down the volume on the phone.

"Faine told you?" I asked. She was usually good at keeping her promises.

"She could not keep the truth from me," he said flatly. "We are next-door neighbors at home *and* in business. When she was acting dodgy during the changeover from dayshift to night as she closed up her café, saying just 'hmm-hmm' when I asked as usual during this trip if she had heard from you instead of her usual bright and cheery, 'She's doing wonderful! Having a great time!' I could not just *stand* there and serve Jeremiah and his farmer peasant ilk their daily booze until I knew what had her acting so strange."

I let out a sigh. I knew how dogged Draven

144

could be when he wanted to know something, so I couldn't blame her. Thinking quickly to check the texts on Cable's phone, I found one from Faine apologizing for letting Draven know because "he was worried." She didn't even smear him, didn't tell the tale he so brazenly admitted to as I read the text, one about following her home and pounding on her door with her children sleeping until she'd fessed up.

"We're fine," I said. Cable grimaced and bit his lip. We were mostly fine. Strange train incidents notwithstanding. But if Draven was acting this way over the car accident—which felt like years ago after this long of a day—I wasn't about to tell him about every other strange thing. "We'll tell you the whole story when we get back tomorrow. We mostly just didn't want Cable's mom to find out. No need to worry her and Milton before we can reassure them in person."

Draven let out a *tsk* but nonetheless grumbled. "Your secret is safe with me." Yeah, because there was no other vampire in town who'd hound someone like that for information. Qarinah, his vampire partner in the pub, was far too demure and respectful of people's boundaries.

"Thank you," I said, trying not to grind my teeth. "We'll be back before sundown tomorrow, so don't worry about it."

"I *will* worry," Draven said, softer this time. So we really *did* need to have the "I've completely and utterly moved on" conversation at some point. But then he elaborated. "I didn't want to worry you and end your excursion prematurely, so I did not tell even Faine, but a week ago, a woman came into First Taste. She asked after you."

Cable and I exchanged a look. A woman? What person outside of Luna Lane even knew I existed but a…

A witch.

"Did she give you her name?" Cable asked.

I could hear Draven's tongue smacking against his fang. Perhaps he'd forgotten my professor boyfriend might have been listening in on this conversation. Despite calling *his* phone.

"She didn't even know *your* name," said Draven. "Not entirely. She asked after Cinnamon Poplar and *her daughter*. I told her I didn't know what she was talking about. Should I have?"

My blood ran cold. Not because he'd done anything wrong, but because it just confirmed I'd been a fool to hope nothing would ever come of Eithne's warning. "No, you did fine. Especially if Eithne was right about witches coming after me." When Mom had fled the rest of the witches to seek shelter with her half-sister, Eithne, the others must have known she'd been pregnant. She'd given birth to me the day after she'd arrived, after all.

But would they have known it was a daughter in particular? I suppose, if even Faine had known months in advance with normie technology, the presumed gender of her children…

"She didn't seem to believe me," said Draven. "But she didn't pry further. After she finished her cocktail, she left. I told Mayor Abdel when he came into the pub the next day, so he and town hall are on alert. He agreed with me to keep the news from spreading around town until your return, though. But now that your trip is at an end…"

"What did this woman look like?" Cable asked.

I chewed the inside of my cheek. Considering Eithne had disguised herself as an elderly woman named "Bette" and flaunted her trickery right in front of my face and I hadn't caught on, I knew witches more skilled than I could hide their appearances.

"Black hair, long. A pleasant face that didn't quite match her demeanor. A little unsure of herself, or unable to handle her liquor." He grew chastising with that remark, as it had been a favorite refrain of his back when I'd had a couple of drinks once in a blue moon. "And striking eyes," he added.

"Striking?" Cable asked.

But I was already thinking that seemed to match one person in particular: Odessa Grimm. An unsteady witch. Was her lack of poise part of some act? Or was a skilled witch capable of general clumsiness?

"Dark brown, so deep, I could have sworn I saw

souls swirling inside there." Draven audibly shuddered.

Brown. Not blue. Unless either time Odessa had used a disguise… At least partially. Her and her children's blue eyes were so striking, I could see a witch trying to camouflage them so they wouldn't stand out at a glance. But a bartender usually got a good look at someone at the pub asking him questions.

Cable let out a sigh and squeezed my knee, his fingers threading through some of Broomie's bristles.

"Thank you for letting me know," I said. I didn't want to worry him about my suspicions and what was going on in the train. "I will keep an eye out."

"It is good you are heading home," he said. "I mean, you deserve to see the world, that is true, but if your curse confined you to Luna Lane for your *protection*—"

"I know," I said curtly, my gaze shifting to the onyx pike leaning between the bench seat and the cushioned toilet seat. Despite the caffeine boost in the dining car, I felt a little out of it. Fatigue was setting in, and the pike looked awfully dull in the fluorescent lighting. Maybe it was just my tired eyes.

Maybe my guilt was starting to catch up with me.

"And now that I know about your accident, I worry… I wonder if this woman, this witch, could have found you and caused it?"

Cable tilted his head. "It was just bad luck. A patch of black ice after rain and a sudden freeze."

My first instinct was to dismiss Draven's suggestion, too.

But if the accident had caused us to board *this* train, where something suspicious was going on…

Then again, Cable and I didn't seem to be the target of any theft. Just the Grimm children's determined curiosity.

An announcement heralded out over the intercom. "Passengers, this is your conductor speaking. Thank you for your patience during our alarm malfunction." Malfunction? But I *knew* the cause of the emergency alarm. "I have to ask that you please make your way back to your seats or roomettes and get ready for lights out. Access granted only to the restrooms. If you need something, hit the nearest *call* button and a staff member will assist you."

We had call buttons on the wall next to the cushioned toilet seat, but we'd yet to use them.

"Did that announcement mention an emergency alarm?" Draven asked. Right. He was on speaker. "Faine said you were coming home on a train, the Speedtracks Overnight Express from Manhattan to Chicago." He really *had* squeezed every last detail out of her.

"There was an incident—" started Cable.

"False alarm," I said quickly over him. "As the conductor said." I pleaded with Cable silently to follow along and he shrugged.

The speaker crackled again. "I know you are all concerned about the thefts earlier this evening—"

"*Thefts?*" shouted Draven.

I opened my mouth to explain or try to downplay it—nothing had been stolen from us, and that was the truth—when my ears felt like they were being squeezed, causing me to lose track of what else the conductor was saying.

"Tunnel!" shouted Cable.

Despite the late hour, the windows apparently *had* let in some source of light from the moonlit landscape and cities we passed through, as now it was eerily black from the window behind me, the harsh artificial light of our roomette suddenly brighter, though it flickered for the next several seconds, too.

We came out of the tunnel and my ears popped in a sort of painful relief.

"Draven, we're fine—oh, the call dropped." I stared at the screen.

"Tunnel," said Cable by way of explanation.

The phone rang again, but instead of answering it and exposing us to more of a harried vampire's lectures, I declined the call and quickly sent the number a text.

We are completely fine, I promise you. We need to get some rest. Big day. See you tomorrow night. Turning phone off until morning.

Which was when Draven would be asleep himself.

I showed Cable the message and then hit *send*.

"I suppose we could actually use some shut eye," he said as the phone rang again. Wincing, he took the phone from me and hesitated, as if to ask permission, and I nodded back. He turned it off.

Cable stood, swaying somewhat with the movement of the train, and grabbed his charger out of his folio bag to plug his phone into an outlet, gathering all of his materials into the bag and stacking it and his phone on top of the cushion seat toilet.

Then he pulled the top bunk out of the wall.

Broomie looked up at his movements curiously.

"You're *serious*?" I asked.

Cable opened the storage compartment and pulled out a pillow and a thin blanket provided by the train. He turned to put them on the top bunk but stopped, staring down at me, his arms full. "You're not tired?"

"It doesn't really matter if I'm *tired*, considering all of the chaos unfolding on this train."

Broomie slid off my lap and floated up to the top bunk, settling down on it. Her brush head poked out to reach the pillow on top of the blanket in Cable's arms and her bristles formed two clumps, gripping the pillow between them. She slowly shifted it toward her on the bunk as Cable spoke.

"The staff is handling it." He let Broomie take the pillow and curl up on it without comment as he arranged the blanket on the bunk. "You're not a police officer, Dahlia. Even if Sherriff Roan keeps relying on you to make sense of all the mysteries in Luna Lane."

"Yeah, when they involve enchantments!" I stood up and pointed to myself, but Cable just used the opportunity to shift the bench cushions aside and turn the seat into the roomette's second bed.

Cable reached into the storage cubby for another pillow and blanket. "We don't know *for sure* there's anything paranormal going on."

I stomped my foot, my boot catching his toe. "Sorry," I said as he winced. "But no, not sorry about the rest of it. Do you not believe me?"

Cable finished making the second bed and grabbed me by both arms. "It's not that I don't believe you. But I'm tired, you *should* be tired, we were asked to stay in our rooms. Don't you think you'll tackle this problem better in the morning if you've had some rest?"

Broomie's soft, bristly snores from the top bunk, the steady lull of the train on the tracks, my sense of weariness... It all seemed to echo Cable's statements.

Sleep. Rest.

Broomie certainly wasn't up for any flying right now anyway. And we'd never chased a train. I wasn't sure how fast it went and if she'd even be able to match pace with it.

We were still fourteen hours from Chicago, another few hours from Luna Lane. I didn't know if she and I could fly all that way if we lost sight of the train.

Certainly not when suffering from lack of sleep, whatever enchantments I cast on us.

Stifling the urge to yawn, I realized not even the coffee was keeping me up for this.

"Fine." Sighing, I turned to the door and said, "KCOL," since the door's lock clearly wasn't up to the task of keeping intruders out of roomettes, even before our door had gotten stuck.

With the enchantment, the door's lock should hold better, at least for a few hours.

So I hoped.

"NAELC," I said, waving my hands over myself. I'd never liked normie showers. I did the same to Cable. I'd done it to him a few times on the road. No laundry for us.

He let out a sigh of relief. "That's convenient."

I felt a little extra unsteady on my feet, and it wasn't just the rocking of the train. I *was* tired and I'd cast a lot of enchantments. Rest would do me good.

"You win." I climbed up into the top bunk. "But I'm getting up early."

Maybe in just a couple of hours.

Even if we *were* supposed to stay in our rooms.

If there was someone paranormal on this train, I was going to find out what they were up to.

Chapter Ten

I woke in the darkness of the roomette as I almost rolled off the top bunk and onto the floor below me, Cable's cries as he also jostled to the side echoing out in my ears.

Broomie chirruped in warning and soared out from the top bunk to float under me, catching me. Cable was less lucky, his head rolling onto the toilet cushion seat beside him and his legs slamming onto the floor.

"What's going on?" he asked, scrambling to his feet. An alarm rang out overhead, just as it had when January had opened the dining car window.

"NO," I said, extending my arms toward the light switch and righting myself on Broomie's back as we lowered slightly so I wouldn't hit my head. The lights flickered on.

Cable was seated at the edge of his bench seat

bed, pulling his glasses out of their case in his folio bag.

"No what?" he asked, blinking. He reminded me of those big men I'd dubbed "pallbearers" and their stony, slow-on-the-uptake looks. But anyone would feel that way roused from the depths of sleep.

"Not 'no,' 'on,'" I explained quickly, sliding down Broomie's back to my feet. "The lights. Why is the train going so fast?"

On unsteady feet, I gripped Broomie for support. The onyx pike clattered back and forth between the bunk and the toilet where we'd wedged it, rattling like an empty, hollow tube.

"I... I don't know," said Cable, his eyes widening.

Something didn't feel right.

The intercom crackled again. "Everyone, this is the conductor speaking. I ask that you remain calm. Please stay seated. If currently in a sleeper car, please get down off the upper bunks at the earliest opportunity and sit up. Hold on to the armrests and *stay* seated."

"That doesn't sound good." Cable worried his lip.

"What time is it?" I wondered. Like that was important right now.

Cable turned on his phone, unplugging it as he did.

"Two in the morning. But there's no service," he said blankly. "Another tunnel?"

I stared outside. We were rounding another curve, and *pineapple broomsticks*, those back cars were *not* taking the curve very well, teetering sideways as they rounded the bend.

"Dahlia, you should sit," he said, making room for me beside him.

"We're going too fast!" I shouted, and the conductor clearly knew it, telling everyone to sit down. "Something's—" I stopped myself.

There. Right before the caboose took that turn, wobbling this way and that as it did so.

The figure on the roof of the train.

"Dahlia…?" Cable asked.

Behind the door leading to the hallway, pounding footfalls indicated a series of people running through the walkways between cars, even if we'd been ordered to stay put.

"I have to go out there," I said, sliding on my boots. Broomie must have seen it, too. Her bristle head nodded. I jumped up on Cable's bed, my toes barely missing his bag, and combed through the overhead luggage compartment to drag my own bag out. "Someone's on the roof." I pulled out my witch's hat, muttered a "SELKNIRW ON" enchantment over it, and placed the black conical hat with its purple band atop my head.

There. I could feel the magical energy all around me funneling through me already.

"Dahlia, I believe you, but why does that mean *you*—" started Cable.

But I'd already pointed my free hand at the window behind him. The alarm would sound if I opened it all the way? Well, it was already sounding. Besides, it might not sound if it stopped existing in the first place.

"Hold on!" I shouted to Cable. "HSINAV WODNIW!"

Cable gripped the armrest of the toilet cushion seat across from him, but I didn't hesitate, the next few seconds moving almost in slow motion as I leaped on Broomie's shaft and slid through the forceful winds.

"Be careful!" shouted Cable at me just as I flicked one hand back toward where the window had been.

"EROTSER WODNIW!"

The window returned just as it had been, and I took note of Cable's tense shoulders slumping, the wind no longer rustling through his hair.

He jumped to his feet and almost tumbled under the quick movement of the car.

But before I could think about it, I was already up, floating high above the train.

The fast, fast-moving train.

"DEEPS!" I shouted into the wind at Broomie, giving her a burst of speed. The train was already almost at the end car beneath us, and there was that figure, wobbling across the train roof.

"Stop!" I shouted, as if the person would listen to me. Broomie was barreling forward, trying to keep up with the train, the wind peeling back my lips as I leaned hard into the wind, flat against my companion broomstick. I couldn't even peel my head up to take a better look at the person.

They'd seemed tall, maybe taller than before when I'd seen them, and on the broader side from one shoulder to the other. Way broader. Like *unnaturally* broader. My first instinct was that it was one of the "pallbearers," but it was too big for even one of them, and there was also an odd protruding hump on the figure's side. About the size of a pumpkin.

And… If I could have moved my head against the force of the wind, I would have done a double take. Did the person have *two heads?*

"POTS!" I shouted, but I could barely move my arm in the force of the wind. I didn't blame Broomie. She was putting her all into keeping pace with the train. My worst fear about the train leaving me behind was compounded now by the thought that I'd be leaving Cable there—on a train full of so many things going wrong. There were other innocents, too.

No, I could *not* fall behind this train.

The figure had not been affected by my enchantment, moving steadily with great, echoing footfalls toward the tail end of the train as if they knew nothing of fear and the speed had no bearing on them. I strained to see in the dark, in the shadow of the night. Could I have been wrong about two heads? What kind of creature had two heads?

Probably something some wicked witch would conjure up to aid her.

"RETSAF!" I said to Broomie, and as if being turbo charged, we skidded in place in the air, only to break free from our position with a burst of speed far beyond what I'd imagined her little body capable of.

"We passed them!" I shouted, fighting the force of the wind to turn my head over my shoulders as we soared over the caboose and toward the observation car, overshooting the figure. I could still barely get a good look, my neck sore. The landscape around us was a blur at this speed, and we were only just now surpassing the speed of the train.

The figure jostled—perhaps they couldn't maintain their balance, either—but then disappeared atop the middle of the caboose. Perhaps there was a hatch there or—was that a third arm, I saw?

Broomie screeched in terror beneath me.

I whipped around.

We were headed for another tunnel.

Broomie tried to correct course, taking us closer and closer to the surface of the observation deck, but she couldn't slow down, not with both of my speed enchantments on her.

I opened my mouth to counteract them, just as the top of Broomie's shaft clonked against the cement of the tunnel's arch and we ricocheted backward to the train below, my head thudding hard against a thick, glass surface.

Someone was petting my forehead, gently brushing my hair off my face.

The back of my head was sore.

"This isn't the first head injury I've seen since we've picked up speed," a woman said. I didn't recognize the voice—or maybe it was vaguely familiar? "What were you two doing in the observation car instead of your room?" She let out a little cry and my body lurched forward.

I was inside the train? And the train still hadn't slowed down.

"Uh, we—" Cable started.

Cable!

I bolted upright, my head growing dizzy.

"Whoa, be careful." That medic I'd seen with the Grimm kids was grabbing me by the arms.

"I'm fine," I said, looking around. Cable and I were in a couple of side by side recliners facing a large window that ran from the floor to the ceiling and all the way to the other side in a big dome. Someone had pushed the armrests dividing the recliners up so I could lean my head on Cable's lap.

My face flushed.

But more importantly… Broomie lay to my side between the back of the recliner and my thigh.

My hands ran over her. Quietly, she let out a bristly whimper.

"Medical to Car 13." The overhead speaker crackled. "Highest priority."

The medic looked up, as if the speaker itself would explain more.

"Just lie here," she said, stumbling as she stood. "Don't make sudden moves. I'll be back."

I didn't have a moment to waste, even if she was still within earshot.

"LAEH," I said to Broomie.

The medic shot me a strange look but gathered her large, black medical bag and made her way on wobbly feet to the next car.

Broomie stretched and cooed as my enchantment took effect. My head *seared*.

"Dahlia," started Cable.

With trembling, exhausted arms that felt like lead, I motioned to the back of my head. "LAEH." I repeated the enchantment all over my body for good measure.

Then I let out a sigh of relief, my energy coming back to me. I looked around.

There were other people scattered throughout the deck, huddled together in recliners, but no one was within earshot or paying us much mind. The train swayed dangerously fast, making it seem impossible to stand. "What happened?" I asked.

"You tell me." Cable's lips pursed in admonishment.

My skin pricked as I was awash with guilt for my foolhardy actions. I caught Cable up to speed.

"Two heads?" he asked in a whisper. "Three arms?"

"At least. I didn't get a very detailed look." Sighing, I swung my feet to the floor and turned to get a better look at the back of the observation car. "Staff Only," a sign read in front of the door leading to the caboose.

A tall man in a staff uniform stood in front of the door, his wrists crossed in front of his pelvis, swaying unsteadily with the movement of the train. There was a scowl on his small-featured face, and I wondered what the staff thought was responsible for all of the problems on the train.

As for myself, I hadn't managed to discover much, but I did know the caboose was where that figure atop the train had gone.

"Wait, how did you find me?" I asked. "And how long have I been out? Has the conductor updated—"

"One question at a time." Cable pet Broomie as she pushed her way between our arms. "It's 2:30—you weren't out long. I raced down the train toward the caboose as fast as I could manage in these conditions." He gestured around him, at the way everyone was wobbling in their seats. "I kept straining to see you, and I wasn't looking where I was going. I ran into that crossword champion at one point in the walkway."

"Rhys?"

Shuddering, he nodded. "He was looking up out

the windows, too. I wondered if he'd caught sight of you, so I asked him what he was looking at, and he told me to mind my own business."

That sounded like Rhys.

"But I couldn't see you, either, from the vantage point of the windows in the passenger cars, so I assumed we were safe. I slid past him, and then I didn't spot you until I got to this observation deck." His gaze tilted upward at the clear dome above us. "And then the tunnel…" Wincing, he looked around. "I would have been surprised no one else seemed to hear the clunk, but the intercom went off just then." I noticed he didn't explain what announcement the conductor may have made just yet, going quiet instead.

"Where was Rhys at that point?" I wondered if he really had gotten a look at me. But what would he assume he'd seen? Or had he seen the two-headed figure atop the train?

"In the observation car with me," Cable said. "Well, closer to the back of it. But I took advantage of the distraction of the announcement and scrambled to the emergency exit." He nodded to the side in front of us, another one of those *Alarm Will Sound* doors. "I could follow Broomie tugging you along the side of the car." He gave her brush head a tousle and she chirped. "She flew up your dress and popped out through your neck hole, dragging you that way."

Scratching Broomie under her vague chin area,

I leaned down to give her brush head a prickly kiss. No one else could see us from here, and so what if they saw me kissing a broomstick? Everyone had more important things to worry about now.

"Thank you, Broomhilde," I whispered. "*No one noticed this?*" I asked Cable.

Cable shrugged. "We'd hit a tunnel. If I hadn't been looking for you, I probably wouldn't have noticed it, either."

"Even Rhys didn't pay you any mind?"

"He wasn't around when I opened the door. I checked. Must have headed back toward the passenger cars." Shrugging a shoulder, he resumed his story about the Broomie-Cable team-up rescue of one foolish, redhead witch. "I pushed open the door as far as the pressure would let me, using my shoe to prop it open." He pointed to his foot. One brown shoe was more scuffed than the other.

"What about the alarm?"

Cable winced. "The alarm was already going off, remember? They hadn't turned it off yet." It was off now, at least.

Hmm. Someone *else* had set off the alarm and used a door or window to get access to the roof? Someone with steady feet and two heads?

I glanced at the staff by the door again. "No one noticed you drag me inside?"

Cable looked around, as if wondering if someone was watching us right now. No one seemed to be.

"The wind was hardly noticeable with the sound of the tunnel and the speed we're going. I don't know. I was too panicked to think straight. I was outside for a bit, and I was hardly paying attention to those in the car. I glanced back when I could, saw the crossword champion walking toward the end of the car again, but he didn't look out at me and that was when Broomie needed me to grab you and take you down off the roof. The whole thing felt like it took forever." He was losing some color to his face, and I felt bad for having ever worried him so. "People may have heard the door slam after I dragged you both inside and grabbed my shoe, but by then, I directed them to your head injury. Said you'd fallen and you had a bump.

"Rhys was walking back toward the passenger car then and I was worried he'd say something, ask where you'd been—I was prepared to tell him you'd headed here before me and I'd found you passed out on the floor—but he left without a word when a few other men offered to help me carry you to the chairs."

Of course the crossword champion wouldn't have helped me when I needed medical attention. He didn't care when kids went flying out train windows.

"Shouldn't have done that. Move you, I mean. Medic said not to move head trauma patients, but I couldn't very well tell her you'd already been moved from down off the roof." He scratched the back of his head with a sheepish expression, then tilted his head slightly toward the caboose. "This guy wasn't here at the time. The conductor posted him there to keep an eye on the back of the train. Most of the staff has been running wild through the cars, best they can manage."

"What was the announcement?" I asked, brushing aside the luck that had let me go undetected. I didn't have the skills to try memory manipulation like Eithne could have done. It felt too invasive—wrong—and I'd never practiced it. That, and I worried I'd mess it up.

"Oh, uh, I was too busy to pay close attention," Cable admitted, "but with all the screams it elicited, I got the gist of it. Basically, we're, uh… stuck…"

"Stuck?" I tilted my head.

"They don't know why the train is running too fast, but they can't slow it down. The brakes aren't working." Cable swallowed. "Apparently, we're in the news." Uh-oh. That didn't bode well, especially with Cable's phone back in our roomette and a brash, worried vampire who'd made it very clear he knew exactly what train we were on. "The train is barreling forward, and other trains have to be rerouted. They're thinking of redirecting us toward a dead-end stockyard, where they're preparing some measures for a softer crash landing, but it'll be hours before we can get the train there. And that's *if* the engineer thinks it's safe to change direction."

That was more than "the gist." Cable's darting glances assured me he'd kept the news from me as long as he could.

Because an out-of-control train that couldn't even brake could only mean one thing.

"The paranormal is involved." I hopped up, gripping Broomie's shaft in one hand and a handrail in the other as the train lurched beneath me, and made my way uptrain.

It was either investigate the medical emergency that had called the medic away or knock out the staff member posted at the caboose and check inside.

For now, it was better that I see if my healing skills could be put to good use.

We left the observation car, headed into a car with a dozen rows of four seats each, split down the middle. People were scattered throughout the car in the seats, though it was hardly packed.

"Quite an evening we're having." The pompous lilt in the voice drew me to look to my left.

Rhys was there, working on—no surprise—a crossword puzzle book open on his lap, his shiny, silver pen dancing across the page. He didn't even look up.

Was this where his ticketed seat was? This far back from the dining room? He struck me as a man who'd want his own quarters. Then again, perhaps he'd never intended to be away from the crossword puzzle event before the conductor had instructed us to return to our seats.

"Did you…" Cable swayed with the train, holding on to the back of Rhys's seat for balance. "Did you ever find out what you were looking at?"

Rhys cocked a brow as he continued to write a word in his book. *Alacrity.* "Pardon?"

"Out the window? Never mind." Cable said the last part louder, quickly covering his previous sentence.

Good idea. Better to redirect his attention from that. Though as the train rocked beneath me, I wondered why Rhys had been walking back and forth so much in the observation car on a runaway train.

I wasn't about to find out.

"You're still out and about, I see, despite the head injury, was it?" He *had* taken note of that. Grimacing, I didn't comment.

"Are we allowed to head back to the dining room then?" Rhys asked. He groaned and clutched his shoulder, but after rotating it a bit, he packed his book into his folio bag and looked up at me.

"Technically, no," I said, eager to keep him here and out of my way.

Wasn't he going to ask why I was walking around with a head injury? And why I'd been in the observation car before Cable, supposedly?

Or had he witnessed what Cable had assured me had gone unnoticed?

"Well, I'll not be the only one left back here on a technicality." Rhys stood, his lips set in a thin, grim line, the black handle I took for belonging to something like a letter opener clacking loudly in his front pocket as he moved, drawing my eye. The pocket bulged just slightly and sagged, like it was overloaded, but I hardly got a second glance before he pushed past me and headed toward the front of the train.

"As if we were off to compete in that stupid contest!" I cried. I waited until Rhys had proceeded to the next car before I took off again.

"Dahlia," said Cable, trying to keep his voice quiet but loud enough to be heard as we pushed our way forward. "I know you want to help—"

He was cut off as I made my way to into the corridor connection. Another car full of just seats. Rhys must have been at the next car already because he wasn't ahead of us. There was another similar car after that, though there were fewer seats in this one because of a bathroom.

Cable tried to talk to me a few times, but I just grunted at him, and he kept quiet. We had over twenty cars to go before we made it to Car 13.

"YDAETS," I thought to say to my feet and then Cable's when we reached the first car with sleeper roomettes, Car 20.

No one was around. I looked over my shoulder, took a deep breath, and held my hands out before me, Broomie gripped in my right. "WOLS,

NIART!" I said. Telling the train to outright stop might have been too dangerous. My energy coursed through my fingers, channeled through my hat, then flowed down through the floor.

And quit.

Like my magic had been a flame blown out by the wind.

"What's wrong?" Cable asked.

I tried again. And met the same resistance.

"Bananaberries," I said.

"You can't slow the train?"

"I thought I'd have better luck inside it than flying overhead…" I shook my head as Broomie let out a sorrowful rustle of her bristles. "Come on, girl. Someone might need our help."

"But you built an escape room from nothing," Cable said as we made our way down the sleeper cars. We continued to not pass anyone else. Other passengers appeared to be better at following directions to stay in their rooms or seats.

"It wasn't from nothing," I said, rolling my shoulders as if to build up strength. But I still wasn't feeling enough energy to push the enchantment harder. "And I had energy-boosting potions." I should have brewed some for the trip. I sighed. "And… No one was working against me."

"So this *is* paranormal?" Cable asked.

"If it weren't, I would have made *some* headway in slowing the train," I guessed.

Cable nodded grimly and we kept moving forward.

Right before we reached the end of Car 14, the crowd gathered ahead in Car 13 visible even through the windows separating the two doors of the cars, Cable grabbed my arm, swirling both Broomie and me around to face him.

His eyebrows drew together as his voice grew deeper. Serious. "Just promise me you'll be careful, okay? I know you're powerful, but I worry about you." His voice broke a little.

I couldn't stay mad at him. All he'd wanted was for me to relax, to let the professionals handle things for once.

But my talents were clearly needed here. And even if nothing had been taken from our roomette during the thefts, between Draven's account of the witch in his pub and this nagging feeling…

I couldn't shake the idea that this was all happening because of *me*.

We made our way to Car 13. Conductor Zapatero was nodding as he spoke to the medic, both clutching the handrail in front of an open roomette door, the light from the door pouring out onto the walkway.

Room 2.

The Grimms'?

"The amount of blood loss indicates a serious injury," the medic was saying as we got closer. "But without the patient to inspect, I can't say—"

Conductor Zapatero took notice of our approach and moved to block our path. "What are you doing out of your room? For your safety, you must—"

"One of my head trauma patients," said the medic, putting a gentle hand on the conductor's chest to give me a better look. She stared at me from top to bottom and frowned, her gaze sticking briefly on the broomstick in my hand, but I supposed that was less of a thing she'd want me to explain than the fact that I was perfectly up and well. Better not to give her a closer look of my head.

"I'm fine," I said. "We were headed back to our room—in Car 12." I jutted my chin in the direction behind them. "But what happened here? Blood loss?"

The conductor scowled at the medic and then reached over her head to slide the roomette door shut. I managed to move forward just enough to get a look. No one *seemed* to be inside. Stuff was scattered everywhere, and that fancy-looking box of Odessa's I'd noticed at the station was open on the bench seat. Something cylindrical, metallic, and reflective on the interior of the box lid caught the overhead light like a camera's flash going off. But more deserving of my attention was the splash of red that extended from the open box and over the pale blue bench seat.

Blood?

"Where are the kids from that compartment?" I asked. "Their mother? Who was hurt?"

The conductor put his back to the door and gestured for me to continue walking. "Ma'am, for your own safety, I must ask that you return to your room—"

"If someone was attacked in that room, I think everyone should know," said Cable, standing up to his full height. He could be intimidating when he wanted to be. It just wasn't in his nature.

"No one was *attacked*." The sentence came out as more of a sigh. "Now, please. You are interfering with an official investigation."

"We'll head back to our room." I grabbed Cable by the wrist and pulled him on.

The corridor connection between Car 13 and Car 12 was as loud as the one just before the dining car, and the short walk was chillier than most of the other connections had been, too.

"What's that?" Cable asked, glancing up. He said something else I missed entirely.

"*What?*" I shouted into the wind, my teeth chattering.

Cable signaled for us to move on, so I did. Once we'd gotten to Car 12, I let him go.

"There was a tear in the ceiling of the gangway," Cable said as we stopped in front of the public restroom.

"The what-way?" I asked.

"The corridor."

That was strange. Then again, the flexible material making up the ceiling of the gaps between cars hardly seemed the sturdiest.

"I'm sure the conductor noticed it. But it's probably just not at the top of his list of worries right now."

He kept looking over his shoulder at the car behind us, then at me, as if to wonder why I was just walking away despite everything I'd done to show I wasn't going to let the strange occurrences on this train go unnoticed.

"We weren't making any headway." I gestured behind me. "Let's get back to our room. Faine and Draven are probably worried—and they may have told your mother by now. You can place some calls and I'll sneak out to do more investigating."

"I don't want you to go alone—"

A toilet flushed from the bathroom beside us.

Cable went quiet at the sound of running water and a paper towel dispenser. I turned on my heel, about to make my way down to our room, when the women's bathroom door opened and out stepped January.

Her brow arched at the sight of us, and though I was relieved to see her unhurt, whatever I suspected her family of, the last thing I'd expected her to do was to reach into the little pocket on the front of her plaid pajama shirt and unfold a piece of paper.

A crossword puzzle. Titled "Special Event 3: Theme: Reaper Calling."

"Nice hat." She scoffed. "I guess you're not hiding it anymore. I solved your message. And I suggest you start talking."

My eyes darted over the filled-in puzzle, circles around some of the usually random words up and down forming a sentence:

Give. Back. Potion. Or. Both. Die.

Chapter Eleven

"*My* message?"

I certainly hadn't encoded any message into an event puzzle. I supposed if, despite everything, Bedwyr was letting the show go on, he would have released the third puzzle at two in the morning.

Were the circled words just a coincidence? He'd had a mystery-themed puzzle before this.

But *potion?*

And what was this child still doing up and solving these puzzles? Despite what had just happened in her own roomette?

I snatched the paper from her and she shouted, "Hey!", going on tiptoes to try to take it back.

It did seem to be a message. Even the hints leading to those six clues had bolded numbers the others did not, as if to draw one's focus to them.

And the theme itself… Awfully inappropriate for

a family-friendly event, even if it had been released in the middle of the night. Bedwyr had assured us we'd all have access to the puzzles we'd missed anytime we dropped in to complete more of the challenges. It was supposed to be family-friendly.

"Where's your mother?" Cable asked softly. Almost as if afraid to hear the answer.

"The dining car," January replied. She crossed her arms. "August is in the dining car's bathroom and it couldn't wait, so I came down here."

The dining car? I lowered the puzzle to look down at the girl and she used the opportunity to snatch her paper back, folding it and sticking it in her pocket.

"The conductor allowed you to stay in the dining car?" I asked, glancing through the windows leading into Car 13. The conductor and medic were joined by more staff now, and he was pointing over their heads toward the back of the train.

"They *kicked* us out of our car, Mother said." She shrugged. "August and I were still in the dining car anyway. The doctor lady told us to stay put when she ran off toward the engine and seemed to forget about us after that. We've been working on our puzzles," she said matter-of-factly.

Cable shimmied his large body to block out the sight of the commotion occurring in front of the Grimms' cabin. "When did your mom join you?"

January's jaw set as she studied him up and down. Then she seemed to give up, relaxing her muscles somewhat. "A while ago. She was cradling her head and moaning about her *potion* causing her headaches. She didn't even care that we were in the dining room. No one told her about the window and"—her bright blue eyes narrowed on me—"no one better."

I shook my head. As if getting the girl in trouble were at the top of my to-do list.

Cable gestured for January to head back toward Car 11.

So if the entire Grimm family was there—if this strange little girl was to be trusted—whose blood was in their roomette?

"August and I aren't getting any sleep," said January once we'd reached Car 11, skipping along the rickety, wobbly walkway as if there were nothing challenging about it at all. "And since that that snooty scar-neck hasn't come back, we're going to catch up and do more puzzles than him."

"Rhys?" I asked her. He hadn't made it back before she'd gone to the bathroom? We passed the elderly ladies' roomettes and the one the pallbearers shared—assuming the three of them could even fit in such tight quarters—and all the doors were closed.

"Whatever his name is." She stopped at the end of the car and swirled around, drawing a line with her finger from the middle of her neck up to her left ear. "I just noticed his thick, creepy scar." Her eyes sparkled, as if she found it delightful.

I bit my tongue and January reached out to pat Broomie by the brush. "Hello, girl," she said to her. "I saw you there, but I don't know if you're good or bad." She set her jaw at me. "But only bad people threaten to murder."

"I didn't—" I sighed, shaking my head. Peering above her into the dining car, I saw that the crossword champion must have returned to his table while January had been in the bathroom. Rhys was back in his seat, this time facing toward Car 11, as he had been at the start of the event.

Odessa and August were at one of the tables—the same one January had nearly flown out of.

Odessa looked haggard, leaning her mouth against her clasped fists, her elbows on the table. I only saw the back of August's head.

"Bedwyr let you leave with a puzzle?" I asked.

Was that why she'd tucked it into her pajama pocket?

January clasped her hands behind her back and rocked back and forth, the tumbling of the train hardly affecting her at all. "I was hoping to confront you with it, but you weren't in your room." She looked up at Cable, then me. "Besides, that judge man hasn't been back to the dining car in ages."

That... made little sense.

January opened the door to the entryway between cars and Cable and I followed, exchanging a quick glance. He'd caught what she'd said, too.

"I'm back!" sang January as she plopped down at the booth beside her brother.

"Please, darling, Mommy has a headache." Odessa's eyes were closed and she massaged her temples.

Rhys let out a snort, his pen flying over the puzzles in what I realized was his own crossword puzzle book again. It was thicker than the one provided for the event, with a red cover as opposed to the event's blue one. Clearly absent was the printed sheet that would denote an event puzzle.

There was a stack of the puzzles on top of Bedwyr's closed briefcase, his mostly-empty coffee cup next to that.

And no sign of the man himself.

"Bedwyr said he had no room or seat on the train," I said to Cable. "That he would be spending the whole trip here in the dining car."

Rhys overheard me and let out something like a growl, never once looking up. "I *wish* that were true so the man would come back." He looked up at me sharply. "Don't you dare take that event puzzle until the proctor has returned." Then he sneered at the children. "As I've told that little boy already. Hopeless, the both of them. *My* child would never act this way."

I couldn't tell if he was being hypothetical or if some poor sap had actually chosen to have a child with this pompous jerk.

August's head sank into his shoulders, the boy

trying to make himself small as he flattened against the window beside his booth.

"You didn't see *me* take one," said January, her little button nose in the air. "You weren't here when I left for the bathroom. Maybe *I* didn't take it." That was a lie.

"He's your twin brother, is he not?" Rhys asked. He muttered under his breath, counting down. Maybe it was a form of meditation.

January shrugged. "Yeah. So?"

"Then you share your twin's burden," Rhys snapped, going back to work on his puzzle book.

I snatched the top sheet of the event puzzle pile atop Bedwyr's suitcase and glared at Rhys as I looked at it.

Theme: Reaper Calling, just as January's had read.

"Who left these here?" Cable asked, peering over my shoulder. I handed him the paper and waited for him to explain.

His finger brushed over the font. "Bedwyr hates Times Roman. Made a big fuss over it at university. This doesn't match the holiday event puzzle we did."

Rhys stiffened and stood, making his way toward us. "Let me see that."

Despite all his harping about cheating, he took a look and frowned. Oh, how he would have gotten along well with a certain ghost in some respects, but she had nothing on the man's dour personality, even if she *had* committed a murder in revenge. Rhys's ears relaxed, as if they'd been tightly clenched along with his jaw, drawing attention to the scar January had mimicked along the left side of his neck.

"This isn't an official event puzzle," he said quickly, taking the paper with him back to his seat. Picking up his pen, he went to quick work, the overhead lights reflecting wildly off his fine-tipped writing instrument as it zipped across the puzzle.

That glint of light. A flash of memory passed through me. A pen like that, lying in a pool of blood on the lid of an open hat box, would have shone just the same.

But it clearly wasn't his. His was right there, all shiny and clean. When would he have retrieved it from under the conductor's nose?

January turned her head slowly, like an owl, almost beyond normie human limits, to glare at me. "*She* put it there."

The accusation brought me back to the moment. "I most certainly did not!"

"Yes, you did." She turned around on the booth completely. "And you're going to kill people, too!"

"If I were going to murder someone, I wouldn't write out a threat in a crossword puzzle and wait for someone to figure it out!" I snapped.

Fatigue was really catching up to me.

"Give. Back. Potion. Or. Both. Die," said Rhys, staring at the paper on his table.

"It wasn't me," I said again, and Broomie nodded her brush head.

Of *course* both January and August were looking, though Odessa still had her eyes closed and Rhys was focusing on the paper.

The children exchanged a devilish grin with one another.

I patted Broomie's head to remind her there were witnesses.

So if the puzzle hadn't been put there by me—obviously—and by Bedwyr, either, who had put it there? And whom was the message for?

Potion… A witch's brew. It had to be. Who had stolen a potion and from whom?

Who would die?

Did that matter, though? Any victim would be too terrible.

The flash of blood on Odessa's seat got me scrambling back to the moment.

I hovered over the Grimms' table.

Odessa didn't even open her eyes, just waved a long-fingered hand at me. She hadn't changed into pajamas, unlike her children. "Finally, you're back. Coffee, please. Maybe a raw egg?"

"I'm not your server," I said. Though that got me wondering. I looked around. No sign of Lien or any of the staff. Though I supposed the conductor had them all running about the train trying to get a handle on whatever was going on.

The train lurched and I slapped one hand on

the table, using Broomie's shaft to steady myself. Even with my "steady" enchantment, this was getting to be too much.

"What happened when Bedwyr came to get you?"

Odessa's eyes blinked open. The blue irises seemed dulled, her movements slow despite the chaos of the speed at which we were barreling through town lights that flickered in blurry streaks out the window.

"What?" Odessa asked simply.

I slammed my palm on the table again. "Bedwyr went to get you around ten… 10:30? Whenever the first alarm went off." I sent a withering gaze toward the kids. As I'd predicted, August slinked back, though January seemed uncowed.

"No one came to get me," she said, reaching for something but finding nothing there. Probably hoping for a coffee cup.

"He did, too. Your kids were in the dining car and—"

"I don't know what to tell you," Odessa said. "I was asleep. I didn't wake up until… until…" Her eyes grew wide, her voice trembling. "The blood. All the blood."

"You were covered in blood?" January asked. She didn't seem disturbed by the idea.

Odessa broke out into sobs, throwing her face against the table in front of her. She sniffled a bit longer as Cable and I swayed in the walkway. Then she leaned back, wiping her eyes, which were running with mascara.

"I try to do right by these little angels," she said. "I'm all they have in the world."

August and January turned to look at me sweetly, as if they were worthy of their mother's descriptor.

"We sunk our last dollar in this trip," Odessa continued. "I have a buyer waiting in Chicago, and the money would be enough to get us back home and pay the mortgage for the rest of the year. But now it's *gone*! And if we even manage to make it to Chicago without being smashed to pieces or murdered"—Cable and I winced in tandem, but January and August exchanged a look of wide-eyed wonder, letting out a little chortle of excitement—"then we'll be destitute."

Cable reached out to pat her shoulder and I sent him a withering look.

This could easily have been an act, for one thing.

"What was taken from you?" I asked. My first instinct was this missing "potion," but why would she tell me she was going to sell it? Unless that was a lie. "What were you going to sell?"

Odessa grabbed a napkin from the dispenser at her table and blew her nose into it. Then she stared at me out of the corner of her eye and finally elaborated. "A brooch. A red-jeweled brooch. It had a Latin idiom engraved on the—"

I found myself handing Broomie off to Cable and then grabbing Odessa by her suitcoat lapels, dragging her down the booth. "Where did you get that brooch?"

Virginia had worn such a brooch before she'd vanished from Luna Lane. My mother had made it for her. It had been meant to *keep her grounded*, in reflection of the Poplar family motto, *Sit tibi terra levis*, or "May the earth rest lightly on you."

"Dahlia, let her go." Cable reached for my forearm, but I turned and snarled at him.

"It's been in the family for ages!" Odessa's voice trembled and she weakly tried to get me to let go. Rather than helping their mother or being horrified by my actions, the kids squealed and clapped.

"Liar!" I said. "Admit it. Admit you're a witch" —January and August gasped, staring at one another with jaws slack—"and you're responsible for stalking me, for everything that's gone wrong on this train ride!"

"Mother, are you a witch, too?" August asked.

"Oh, please, please, please," added January.

Odessa's breaths were ragged, her chin trembling as she looked up at me with bulging, blue eyes.

She was either an exceptionally good actor— which maybe a skilled witch *would* be if "Bette" had been any indication—or genuinely terrified. Of me.

Bette had never been terrified. Eithne had never let any weakness show, even as an "innocent" old lady.

Slowly, my fingers unfurled, letting go of Odessa's coat, and the woman sunk back into her seat.

"I don't know what you're talking about," she said, shirking back from me. As if *I* were the odd one here. Which, okay, maybe, if I was wrong. *If.* "I've never met you in my life before yesterday."

"I told you she was a witch!" shrieked January. Her eyes darted greedily to Broomie in Cable's hands, and I snatched my companion broomstick back. "*She* did this to the train! She stole from everybody!"

I wasn't used to being on the receiving end of accusations. "I did not! I *am* not," I added belatedly, clearing my throat as my eyes darted guiltily toward the broomstick in my hand, tugging on the brim of my conical witch hat to hide my shame. Had I gotten this so wrong? If only I could have brewed some potions for clarity, to get Odessa to speak the truth. I couldn't be wrong. She *had* to be a witch.

Behind me, amidst the loud clank of the train wheels beneath us, the bottles behind the counter clanking with the sheer speed every few seconds, there was a distinct rustling of papers.

I turned to find Rhys standing over Bedwyr's briefcase. It was open, and he was rummaging through it. The lining seemed heavier than it had before. Lumpier. Almost about to break with all the jostling Rhys was doing.

Someone snatched my hand and I whipped

around to find January clutching it. "Oh, please," she said. "Make me a witch, too. I don't mind you being wicked. Really! I was just testing you when I talked about good and bad. I was smart enough to figure out your message, and I would take ever-so-good care of my very own adorable pet broomstick, so please."

Broomie chirruped in my hand.

"Me, too!" said August from beside her.

"*Boys* can't be witches," she spat over her shoulder. His face fell.

Cable lightly pushed past me toward Rhys. "What are you doing? You can't rifle through his stuff. You shouldn't have been able to open—"

"I watched him unlock it several times," said Rhys simply. He took his pen and stabbed at the bulging fabric lining. "For a brain like mine, it was simple to remember the combination." He tapped his temple with his pen, then tucked it behind his right ear as he shifted aside to let Cable through. The skin beneath that ear was unblemished.

Cable reached for the briefcase. "That doesn't mean you should—"

With a clunk, something fell from the briefcase to the ground, the upper lining of the briefcase swinging downward, revealing a hidden compartment.

"As I suspected," Rhys said, standing tall and straight. Cable bent over to pick up the fallen object, his balance unnaturally steady in the fast-moving train due to my enchantment.

He held the object up. It was relatively small, about the size of an egg, and it shined in the overhead light, crystal clear jewels embedded in silver and red.

"My brooch!" cried Odessa. Scrambling to her feet, she shoved me aside, breaking January's grip on me as she tore the object from Cable's hands.

Her eyes lit up as she held it up to the light. "*Ad astra per aspera*," she said, reading something that must have been engraved on the silver of the brooch.

"'To the stars through adversity,'" Cable translated.

Not the Poplar family motto at all.

"Oh, thank you!" She embraced Cable, though he had hardly played a role in discovering it at all.

Rhys returned to his seat, nodding, then took hold of his pen again to get back to work on his own personal puzzle book. "The thief was clearly Bedwyr Hamdi."

Odessa stepped back from Cable, though the force of the train sent her careening back. "That scum!" she said.

"Wait, wait, wait…" Even with my steadying enchantment, the rocking of the train was getting a bit much. I stepped backward until I could sit on a stool at the counter. "Bedwyr was *here* when the thefts occurred."

"Must have had an accomplice," Rhys said simply, not looking up from his book. "Then they hid the stolen items in his briefcase."

Cable frowned as he steadied Odessa and directed her to sit in the chair Bedwyr had often used.

"Is there anything else in there?" I asked Cable. He winced. Now was not the time to worry about digging through his colleague's things without permission.

Odessa had no such compunction. She rifled through the secret compartment. "An empty cologne bottle," she said. "And a letter opener." She shuffled through the papers, sending them flying across the table and hitting the empty plate on Bedwyr's table, which slipped off the table and shattered. Out of "do-gooder" habit more than anything, I crouched down to pick up the pieces and saw a tea cup shattered on the floor beneath the table as well, a pool of tea collected against the edge of the wall. Perhaps it had fallen earlier due to the train's unsteadiness.

By Rhys's feet was also a perfectly whole scone. Rhys let out a grunt and used his foot to kick it behind him and out of my view.

Sor-ry. I stood and put the pieces I'd managed to grab on the countertop. They slid off behind the bar almost immediately. *Oops.*

"What else was stolen?" Cable asked. He picked

up the black letter opener and weighed it in his hand a moment before handing it over to me.

"The ladies never said," I pointed out, the opener heavier in my grip than I'd expected it to be. The edges were dull, but they didn't seem dull enough to be safe for opening letters. And the very tip looked a bit *too* sharp. "And I'm not sure if any other people on the train had things stolen." Nonetheless, there was something about this letter opener that bugged me. "All of those doors were open—"

"Though nothing was taken from our room," added Cable.

Rhys slammed his pen down on the puzzle book in front of him and massaged his temples. "Perhaps the thieves were only looking for things of value. Whatever the case, we have a suspect. Report it to the conductor and let him deal with it." Letting out a groan as he cradled his shoulder a moment, he stood, gathering his things into his folio bag. "Since it is clear the event is over, I have no reason to be out here solving puzzles when not under a judge's watchful eye." His fingers grazed the paper with the clearly fake puzzle. It was half-solved. He put that in his bag, too.

"Good day," he said, though it was three in the morning by now. Shuffling past Cable, he headed back toward Car 11.

"Letter opener…" I murmured to myself. Then I remembered. I was about to follow after Rhys, to ask him if he'd lost his—at least that was what I'd thought I'd seen in his pocket earlier—but as he opened the door to the next car with a thunderous echo of wind, I caught sight of the dull black handle jabbing into his lapel.

So it wasn't his?

This one *was* shinier. It had some heft to it, too, and it would have been awkward carrying around in a breast pocket. If I didn't know better, I might have thought it was… onyx. But that would have been a strange coincidence.

Cable picked up a piece of paper from Bedwyr's briefcase and drew my attention back to him. "This is the *real* event puzzle three," he said, looking at it. "Theme: Animals."

January turned around in her booth and flexed her fingers out in the air, stretching her arm almost as far as it would go. "Let me have it."

Odessa let out a little laugh. "Darling, the event is over. And now that we have the brooch back, we don't really need the free train fare."

January kept flexing her fingers unabated, and Cable handed her the paper.

"I told you *she* brought the fake puzzle," January said, reaching across her brother to pick up a pencil where it had rolled against the wall.

"Me, too!" August pleaded to Cable.

Cable took another sheet of paper and handed it to the boy.

Rolling my eyes, I ignored January's accusation

—I knew I had done no such thing—and made my way over to Cable and Odessa.

Odessa shirked back, clutching her brooch to her chest, but I got a good view of it between her manicured fingers. It looked nothing like Virginia's enchanted brooch from my mother. There were diamonds on it, and the shape was all wrong.

Could I have been so wrong about Odessa?

I glanced back at her children, hard at work at their puzzle.

Were they really just weird? If they were good actors, surely, they would have striven for personas less… conspicuous.

I rested my chin atop Broomie's brush head, wondering what my focus on the Grimms had made me miss. I'd only wanted to help, to combat whatever paranormal forces were at work here—and there was no doubt in my mind that there was something of that nature afoot—but so far, I'd done little more than get myself knocked out and accuse a potentially innocent woman of witchcraft.

A witch was a wicked thing to be, if Eithne were to be believed. She'd insisted my mother and I were the only kind-hearted witches around. Given her own participation in a few foul deeds—despite her obvious love for my mom and even me, I supposed —I'd have to agree.

"Dahlia," Cable said softly, lifting two items from the briefcase.

At first glance, I could see why Odessa had described the one item as an empty cologne bottle.

But for all the time he spent around my own living room, adorned with potions and brewing ingredients, Cable would know as well as I did.

This was an empty potions flask.

Chapter Twelve

"Why are you looking at that piece of junk like that?" Odessa asked. She leaned forward to get a closer look at the flask and then the letter opener I held in my hand. "Are those *worth* anything? The other items stolen? Well, he used up or spilled whatever pricy cologne was in that bottle, sorry to say."

Were these the other items stolen? What did that mean? And who else but Mr. Snootnose bothered to travel with a valuable letter opener?

But *was* it a letter opener? I pricked the tip of my finger on the tip and yelped at the bead of blood that formed there. It seemed more like a genuine dagger to me.

"Are you all right?" Cable asked.

I nodded, sucking on my finger to stop the blood and exchanging the dagger for the bottle. Could either of these things have been taken from Sally, Dora, and Mabel?

The empty flask smelled familiar. I'd smelled this before, and not too long ago. Hints of... daisy?

This dagger... Was it truly made of onyx? Would this work as well as my unwieldly pike to end a witch's life if I needed it to?

My palm felt clammy.

If I *had* to. Only if I had to. Surely, Eithne had been exaggerating about how much more wicked the other witches could be. And my importance to them.

A royal with the blood of a gargoyle golem. Tainting the royal bloodline. But I was also perhaps the last witch princess left, now that Eithne and my mom were gone.

Odessa stood on shaky legs, clutching her brooch tightly to her chest. "We have to tell the conductor, have the staff search for this thief now that we know he took everything." She gazed around. "Where *is* everyone who works here?"

Sliding the empty flask into the pouch at my belt, I looked around for a place to hide the dagger, but it wasn't going to fit in the pouch. With Odessa's back turned, Broomie chirruped, her brush head grabbing the onyx dagger from me and hiding it amid her bristles.

"Dealing with the train out of control, I assume," Cable offered. Almost as if on cue, the sound of a helicopter's blades from above drew everyone's eyes upward, as if we could see through the solid ceiling. Well, I probably would have been able to, if I cast an enchantment and there weren't so many witnesses who didn't need additional proof of their suspicions.

"Media?" Cable suggested. "Or part of the plan to stop the runaway train?"

Tap, tap, tap. There was a small clunk somewhere against a window, almost like the sound of branches scraping against glass in the wind.

An annoyingly familiar shrill alarm went off, just as a burst of wind shot through the dining car, sending Odessa flat against the window opposite in front of us.

"Children!" she shrieked.

January and August were at the "open only in case of emergency" window beside them, one or both of them having opened it again in what was certainly an emergency but not the kind that called for open windows just yet.

Bananaberries. Who'd believe them if they saw me cast enchantments anyway?

"ESOLC WODNIW!" I shouted, forcing one arm through the wind.

Something flapped and fluttered above my head, but it wasn't until the window slammed shut and the force of the wind died down that I realized what I was hearing.

The twins jointly uttered, "Whoa" and stared at me, slack-jawed.

A bat. Above my head.

Cable adjusted his glasses as he peered upward. "Draven?" The bat flapped until it hovered just in front of us in the walkway.

It couldn't have been. We were still… I didn't know, the speed had probably messed with the amount of time we had left until we hit Chicago—perhaps *literally* hit Chicago—but we were far too far from Luna Lane. And at the rate we were going, *no* vampire or even bat should have caught up to us perfectly like that and tapped on the window. It had to be a coincidence, a—

With a *poof*, the bat transformed into Draven, his heavy-booted feet landing with a thud on the walkway in front of me.

Long, blond hair, deathly white skin, steel gray eyes rimmed in red, and a trim if well-defined body partially hidden beneath a black leather jacket with a wide lapel, perfectly matching his black leather pants.

Odessa screamed and fell back into the chair.

The twins gazed at one another, their slack jaws not moving an inch. "*Whoa*," they said again.

"*Draven!*" I shouted. "Have you lost your mind?" I gestured around him at Odessa and the kids.

Draven turned his head just slightly, his body moving gently with the rocking of the train, to stare down at Odessa. He smiled, revealing his protruding fangs.

She shrieked and then fainted, slumping over in her chair. Cable pushed past me to check on her.

"There is clearly something wrong on this train," Draven said, as if he hadn't just flown over here in his bat form for miles. I supposed he didn't breathe, so there was no way he'd get winded.

"You *think?*" I gestured at the rate of speed the scenery was going by in the dark outside. "How did you…? What do you…? Why…?" I massaged my forehead. Then a more pressing thought jumped to the forefront of my mind. "What time is it? How are you going to make it back to your coffin in time?"

"It is half past three," he said, as if there were nothing for him to worry about in the slightest. He did keep some kind of internal track of the hour, considering he had to be in his coffin by daybreak. As if to undermine his cool demeanor, though, his eyes squinted in the harsh overhead lights. He normally preferred dim lights. "I can fly *very* fast."

"Apparently." That would explain how he'd caught up to us, with the distance between us and Luna Lane and the speed. It had taken all of Broomie's and my might combined to match pace with this runaway train.

"She's okay," said Cable, stepping back. I'd almost forgotten about Odessa. "Breathing, anyway. Should you heal her?"

I glanced at Odessa and shook my head. Perhaps it was best she sleep for this one. "Just make sure she's comfortable."

January appeared behind Draven and tugged on a bit of his leather sleeve. "If I let you drink my blood, can I become a vampire, too?" She shot me a glare. "*She* won't make me a witch."

Draven took in the sight of the child and grinned roguishly. "I like this kid. Great aesthetic."

August popped up from the booth behind January.

"They're a pair?" Draven exclaimed. "Excel-lent." Then he turned back to me. "I see you were not so worried about these children discovering your secret? What does it matter if they know mine?"

"It matters because I haven't *confirmed* I'm a witch in front of potentially normie kids."

"*Normie?*" said January, her nose twitching.

"Poten-tia-lly?" August echoed slowly.

"Ah, I think you just did confirm it," Cable pointed out, entirely unhelpfully.

Correctly, but unhelpfully.

Draven turned to January and gave her a pat atop her black-haired head. "I do not make vampires," he said. "I have made this promise to my mummy mayor."

"Your mother is a mayor?" August asked.

"No, no. My mother, she died hundreds of years ago in Transylvania. She was never a vampire. My mummy mayor is the walking undead. A wrapped mummy from Egypt."

I slapped my face with my free hand.

"And a witch cannot make another witch like

you think," Draven added. "A witch is born a witch. Your mother would have to be a witch—"

January pointed at Odessa, her finger trembling. "But the redheaded witch said our mother *is* a witch!"

Draven's blond eyebrows narrowed on Odessa's prone form. "Is she?" he asked me.

"Does she look familiar?" I asked. "I thought she might be the witch you described."

Draven shook his head. "Unless she was in disguise. But this witch who came into my pub, she was of Asian descent, with bright, beautiful brown eyes."

He could have told me that earlier. Not that it mattered when I supposed a witch could transform into almost anybody—

I whirled on January. "You keep saying you saw *me* put those fake crossword puzzles on top of the briefcase?"

"Yes." She looked to her brother. He nodded. "We both did. I said something to you, but you *sneered* and walked back to the sleeper cars."

"I do *not* sneer," I sneered.

Cable cleared his throat.

Maybe I *had* lost some of my composure around this child before.

"Well, it wasn't me," I said, wiping my clammy palm against my skirt.

"The real second witch," said Cable, almost reverently. "She disguised herself as *you*? But why?"

"To hide her own identity." My gaze still flicked to Odessa. *She* wouldn't want her kids to know it was her if they weren't aware she was a witch. But as soon as I thought it, I realized I'd been barking up the wrong tree.

I stared at January and August. They were just weird kids with a love for the spooky and strange.

The brooch being unrelated to the Poplar family crest had helped cement that.

I'd been so focused on this family, I'd been ignoring every other possible suspect.

The figure on the train had had two heads that second time I'd seen them—but they'd been larger than the two Grimm children combined. It wasn't like they'd been clutching to each other, walking along the train roof…

I let out a gasp.

"Dahlia?" Cable asked, almost at the same time Draven asked, "What is it?"

Maybe it *had* been two people side by side. I hadn't really gotten a good look at them.

Now that I knew I wasn't looking for an obvious paranormal monster, that opened up a whole lot of possibilities.

"Odessa's right," I explained. "Where *is* every-one? Even if they're dealing with the chaos, the engine car is that way." I gestured behind Draven. "And we know the conductor is that way." I pointed behind me. "He hasn't once been rushing back to the engine during all of this chaos?"

Cable bristled. "Well—"

The lights overhead flickered then cut off, and we barreled forward through a tunnel, the darkened landscape being replaced with the pure black of solid wall.

"Tunnel!" said Cable, clutching to the table behind him. Even with the steady enchantment, he was losing balance.

"NO STHGIL!" I shouted, but the lights didn't come on. Again, my powers pushed up against something blocking it. It wasn't like the loss of power I'd experienced before. It was more like my power was *up against* something else. An equal force.

The children let out a mixture of giddy screams and sheer terror, their forms tumbling toward the booth they'd vacated. Then the lights went out entirely, plunging us all into pure nothingness. The door behind me whipped open, the sound and the force of the air current hard to ignore even if I couldn't see a thing.

"Watch out!" cried Draven. Right. His eyesight wouldn't have been impeded by the night.

With a pop and a sudden flapping of wings, one grazing my hat and causing me to fix it on tighter, Draven soared over my head toward the open door.

"SEYE ERIPMAV." I gestured at my own face.

My eyes grew tight, like they were suddenly very dry, but I blinked, and everything around me came into focus.

Only it wasn't as clear as it would have been

under the light of day. More like my eyes had adjusted to the darkness much faster than they otherwise would have on their own. A figure retreated back to Car 11 and Draven in bat form fluttered and pushed himself forward into the gust of wind.

"What's that smell?" asked Cable. I whirled on him and he let out a yelp. "Dahlia, you have glowing red eyes!"

I caught sight of the red-rimmed irises in the darkness in the reflection of the window behind him. There was also something else. Something red and pulsing in the dark, running throughout my body in the mirror image. I looked around. The red lines were present throughout the bodies of everyone in this room.

Blood.

Was this how Draven and the other vampires saw us? As the blood flowing through our veins first and foremost?

I shook my head. Didn't matter. I could see and I'd *need* to see if the lights weren't coming on anytime soon. Even though we'd passed through the tunnel and the landscape offered a semblance of meager light, I could see everything in much sharper detail with my transformed eyes.

"Just temporarily." I supposed there were a number of ways I could have made it easier for me to see, but "vampire eyes" had been the first thing to pop in my head. "Check on the kids!" I shouted.

"WOLG!" I stuck out one hand to light the way for him.

Cable got up from where he'd been plastered against the window and stumbled toward the children. Maybe I'd need to cast another "steady" enchantment once we—

But what was that?

Cable was right. A strange scent invaded my nostrils just as a fine, red mist seeped into the glowing light of my hand.

"Are you hurt?" Cable asked over the force of the wind, sliding in beside the kids at their booth. They shook their heads, but as Cable moved to open his mouth, the mist reached their table, pushing beyond it and uptrain, and all three of them slumped over.

"Cable?" I asked, taking a few steps forward.

I shook Cable's shoulders with my glowing hand while Broomie poked her brush head at August's and January's backs. They were all breathing, but it was like they were sleeping.

A sleeping enchantment?

The color had reminded me startlingly of para-paranormal, the substance formed from the meeting of two kinds of dark magic and a sacrifice—the death of an unwilling victim—but that had been odorless, and its mere proximity had stolen away my magic. It had been gel-like, too, not evaporated into mist.

"NOITCETORP." I waved a hand over Cable

and the children, then repeated the enchantment for their mother at her table. No one should come up to them and harm them any further. But perhaps it was best they stayed asleep, so Draven and I could face whatever paranormal threat was headed our way.

Draven!

"YDAETS," I repeated to my feet to give myself an extra boost of stability before running through the open car door, using magic to shut it behind me and proceeding into Car 11.

There was no sign of a bat or another mysterious figure in front of me, no open roomette doors or passing staff.

Just the red, red mist permeating every inch of the train car.

A red mist that didn't affect me—maybe didn't affect Draven, or I might have come across his sleeping form by now.

Perhaps it only affected normies.

I moved on to Car 12. Same story. When I got to my room, I looked to Broomie. She turned her brush head to me curiously, a little sliver of the onyx dagger she held glistening in my vampire-sight.

Could I trust that to be enough? To actually work against a witch? I didn't know for *certain* what it was, where Bedwyr or whoever had framed him had gotten it.

I opened the door to my roomette. It wasn't locked. Cable had run out of here in a panic. I reached for the onyx pike we'd wedged between the toilet seat and the bench seat, though it had jostled in the quick movements of the train. I grabbed it.

It… felt wrong.

I picked it up. It was far too light. I even checked my left arm to make sure I hadn't grown back my stone scales to account for the way it hardly strained me to move it.

Nope. Flesh and blood.

Broomie chirruped and whacked the pike with the bottom of her shaft. It echoed out hollowly.

Hollowly. This wasn't my onyx pike!

"ERUTAN EURT RUOY LAEVER!" I said to the hollow pike, knowing that without any potions and without my rune circle, I would have a difficult time getting an enchanted item to budge if the witch who'd cast the enchantment had intended for its transformation to be undetectable.

But it shrank and transformed quickly in my hand.

I was holding a wooden knitting needle, unadorned and light cedar wood.

Of course! Dora, Sally, and Mabel—how could I have not seen it? They weren't the young, knockout versions of witches Eithne and my mom had always been—and Eithne at least had been several centuries old—but what did that matter?

Witches could disguise themselves. Or maybe some witches chose to grow old.

How would I know?

All I knew about witches was what Eithne had told me.

They were wicked—more wicked than she.

And they were out for my blood.

The fact that there were *three* of them on this train now…

Even with Draven, I was outnumbered. And I couldn't find him just now.

Outnumbered. Targeted. Barreling toward a dead end at high speeds I couldn't curtail.

And now I didn't even have my onyx pike.

Chapter Thirteen

would have to pray the letter-opener-like dagger would do. Right now, I had a vampire to catch up to. I didn't know how much he could help, but a vampire *could* drink the blood of a witch. I knew that firsthand. Maybe he could keep drinking until she—they—passed out.

I'd have to keep the other two distracted, of course.

Our odds of success were low, but I wasn't going down without a fight. Not unless I could get them to leave everyone else on this train alone.

Tossing the knitting needle onto the bench seat, I took Broomie out into the hallway, then, deciding to throw caution into the wind, I mounted her.

"Let's go," I told her, directing her to glide me along the train walkway. I lifted my hand every time we met a door, shouting, "NEPO, ROOD!" just in time so we could glide right through.

A few more sleeper cars of empty walkways and we hit the cars with the passengers in seats. The red mist hung over the air, and they were all fast asleep, too.

"Conductor Zapatero!" I pointed out to Broomie as we flew past him and a number of the staff strewn collapsed in the walkway between rows of seats. My vampire eyes showed the blood flowing, so I had to hope they were okay. But I didn't see Draven in either humanoid or bat form, so I had to keep going.

In the car before the observation deck, I spotted another familiar face.

Rhys Aloveius, the crossword champion, was slumped over in his seat, an open puzzle book in his lap and his hand still clutching a pen poised over the half-completed puzzle. His head lolled back, his glasses askew, the scar traveling up his neck and left ear glowing bright red in my vampire sight. Only…

"Broomie, wait!" I cried out. She screeched to a stop and I jumped the couple of feet to the ground, putting my fingers on his neck.

"No pulse," I told Broomie. "He's dead."

His puzzle book slid to the chair beside him in a particularly bumpy movement of the train, its red cover distracting to my vampire sight.

I gazed around the room at the other passengers. Blood flowed, the pulsing sign of life. Just Rhys, then. Had he had a bad interaction with this fine red mist?

Or had someone murdered him since I'd seen him last?

A crash from the direction of the next car over drew my attention. I would have to figure out what had happened to Rhys later.

"NEPO, ROOD!" I said to the next two doors, floating into the observation car on Broomie's back once more.

There were more passed-out passengers scattered throughout the car here, their blood pumping as the red mist swirled overhead.

The door to the caboose was wide open, the slight fluttering of wings echoing out amidst all the other noise. And the thumping, like someone was dropping rocks every minute or so.

I soared into the caboose and found Draven popping into his humanoid form, then back to his bat form to dodge someone's lunging attack.

Yet there was no blood flowing in this figure, either. But it was clearly moving—and attacking my ex-boyfriend.

"POTS!" I said, waving my arm at the tall figure.

It froze, giving Draven enough time to turn back into his humanoid form, stumbling over the large, open trunk he'd been floating over.

I blinked, trying to bring the assailant into focus. But before I could, someone else moved behind Draven, just as large and overpowering.

"Watch out!" I cried, unable to quite make out

this creature, either. The blood flow that marked normies was absent, my vampire eyes feeling almost a hindrance amongst these attackers who could hide in the shadows without a sign of life.

Draven struggled, his own flesh devoid of the trailing pumping of blood, so following him was proving equally difficult for me.

"WOLG," I said again, my hand letting out a light that traveled across the caboose packed to the brim with luggage as I searched for them. There was a curtain drawn toward the back, piles of luggage around it, barely leaving any room to maneuver, though there was just enough room to slip behind it. The open trunk Draven had stumbled over—I recognized it as the one those pallbearers had carried.

No wonder they had traveled so slowly with it over their shoulders. It was full of rocks, small boulders about the size of my head.

Someone's large hands reached into the pile of boulders and flung the rock. I followed the path of the rock, and just as it was about to hit Draven's head—he was hissing at the large man swinging at him, and I wasn't sure he noticed it—I shouted, "LLAF!" and motioned at the small boulder. It fell straight to the ground with a thud.

Draven turned on his heel, squinting into my glowing light, and offered me a nod of gratitude.

The man attacking him took advantage of this moment of distraction and lunged forward, revealing himself clearly to me in the light. It was one of the "pallbearers," his expression as blank as if he were taking a peaceful stroll even as his body moved with menace.

"POTS!" I waved a hand at him, barely balancing atop Broomie's back, and he froze.

My other, glowing hand swept over the rest of the caboose. The first "pallbearer"—or "rock bearer," was more like it—whom I'd enchanted to stop was still frozen as well, so that made two. But then there was the third one, who had tried and failed to throw the latest rock.

A boulder sailed toward the air again, clipping Broomie's brush and sending us spiraling the couple of feet to the caboose floor.

"Dahlia!" shouted Draven.

A distinct skittering sound echoed out below me and I realized Broomie had dropped her hold on the dagger. Thanks to my glowing hand, I could see it skitter several yards in front of us.

"Broomie, are you okay?" I asked her, lifting her head. Her bristles were splayed out, as if permanently bent. She let out a chirrupy moan. "LAEH," I said, and her bristles righted. She shuddered in relief.

"Behind you!" Draven called with a hiss.

I spun in place on the floor, my arm waving to fend off the attack, my mouth casting out for the first enchantment that came to mind.

"TRAP!" I wanted Draven and his attacker

parted so Draven would be out of danger, the attacker as far away from either of us as I could send him.

Instead, my hand made an arc across the caboose, and it was the curtains at the back that shifted aside.

I only just had time to make out Rhys—hunched over and working on a puzzle book, the scar trailing up the right side of his neck bright red in my vampire vision—before Draven's little batty squeal rang out, another boulder soaring straight for my head.

Chapter Fourteen

I leaned sideways, just in time to avoid the flying boulder, which landed behind me with a thunk. My gaze and enchanted glowing light darted wildly toward Rhys, just enough to take in his smug face focused, as usual, on the puzzle book in his lap despite the chaos unfolding around him. The large, open suitcase by his feet was empty, but I didn't have time to marvel at that or how he'd passed by from behind me without me noticing—or the fact that I *still* wasn't seeing the blood flowing in his veins, when he was clearly alive and alert—because another boulder went flying toward me.

"POTS!" I said, rolling out of the way and turning my attention to the pallbearer. This time, I hit him successfully and he froze in place.

Panting, I waved my glowing hand around the caboose interior. All three pallbearers were still, as silent as statues.

I'd enchanted them to stop, but not to turn into stone. I hadn't used a "freeze" enchantment or anything, but these men weren't so much as blinking.

A little squeak drew my attention, the graveling scribble of Rhys's pencil across his paper nearly but not entirely drowned out by the loud whoosh of the train car beneath us. I scanned the interior of the caboose with my glowing hand until I saw Broomie floating by me, pointing out the source of the little squeaking. It was coming from the open trunk these giant men had carried onto the train.

The one full of rocks.

I scurried over there, peering inside. Little Draven bat lay on his back across one boulder, a tear in his trembling wing membrane.

I snatched him up with a gentle grip, my mouth opening to cast a healing enchantment, when I let out a little squeak of my own instead.

My vampire eyes saw the pumping of blood in the gaps between the stones piled in the trunk.

But Draven first. "LAEH." The little membrane in his wing knitted back together seamlessly.

The fuzzy little bat righted himself on my palm, then took to the air, poofing back into humanoid form beside me.

Broomie wrapped around his shoulders and nudged his flawless white cheek with her bristles.

He pet her back, his black nail polish stark

against his long, white fingers in the light I shined at them.

He jostled backward slightly. "Please, direct the light away from me."

Come to think of it, my vampire eyes didn't seem to like staring at the light too long, either.

"I like what you've done with your eyes." He smirked.

I shook my head despite the grin forming on my face and turned my attention back to the open trunk.

"SKCOR, EVOM," I said, waving my hands over the surface.

The rocks shifted aside, revealing the source of the pumping, thriving blood.

As well as a corpse without a sign of life to it.

"Lien?" I asked, shaking her by the shoulder. She was curled up, face to face, with the still form of Bedwyr. He was the one without blood flowing.

Draven gasped as he knelt over the side of the trunk to look inside. I thought the sight of the dead man must have shocked him for a moment—though why he, an undead, would care so much about a stranger's dead body...

"This is the witch," he said. "The one who asked after you in Luna Lane."

"What?" I shifted her aside so he could get a better look at her face, shining my glowing hand over it. She was still clutching what appeared to be an empty doggy bag against her thigh, a lidless Styrofoam cup at her feet. "Her?"

"Yes," said Draven. "I'm sure of it."

"She's alive at least," I said, crumpling back to the floor. My brain was trying to piece together everything, getting over the shock of Bedwyr not having that thriving flow of blood. But then again, neither had Rhys, and he was alive. I shot back up and checked Bedwyr's pulse.

No. Nothing.

My insides deflated. What had become of the man?

Unless… My gaze darted over the darkness. No one in here but Lien and I *had* flowing blood. Not Draven, not Rhys, not the three attackers.

"The event judge is not among the undead," said a voice carrying across the large space. Haughty, hard to pin down, but something like a subdued Irish or Welsh. "He's well and truly dead." The scratching of his pencil across the paper made me shine my glowing light toward Rhys.

Still doing his puzzle, like the cursed with a one-track mind.

With… a pencil instead of a pen for once. Where was his shiny, silver pen now?

Leaping to my feet, I made my way across the caboose, shimmying around the small space to take hold of that infuriating puzzle book from the man's lap.

"Time to tell me what you know——" I started,

but I wasn't succeeding in taking the book away from him.

He grabbed it and yanked hard, a growl emitting from his throat.

"You're cursed," I said.

He yanked the puzzle book back. "If you know that, don't try to stop me."

I stared at him, his ceaseless completing of the puzzle, his almost single-minded focus. "You *can* stop doing puzzles," I told him. "I've seen you come up for air on occasion."

He snorted and his pencil kept moving.

"When you boarded the train," I continued, my eyes darting to the large, open, and empty suitcase beside him. It was the one he'd been dragging behind him, the one that had seemed so heavy, the wheel had wobbled with the effort it had taken him to move it. "And in the dining car once in a while. Making your way back and forth there..." I stopped.

So *what* had been so heavy in the suitcase and where were its contents now?

"You're not human," I pointed out.

I had to get him talking. If he knew what had happened to Bedwyr... Had *he* knocked Lien unconscious? Even though she was a witch?

The red mist was absent in this caboose car, I realized as I took in a breath devoid of that sickeningly sweet taste.

So she hadn't been knocked out by the mist
regardless.

"I am a human," he said. "I *was*," he added, not
looking up from his puzzle book.

I looked over my shoulder. I could just make out
Draven's form in the darkness.

"A vampire?" I asked.

Both Rhys *and* Draven let out a *tsk* at that. Now I
knew why Rhys had rubbed me the wrong way. He
shared all of Draven's terrible traits and none of his
good ones.

"He is no vampire," said Draven simply. I didn't
ask how he knew; even borrowing a set of vampire
eyes, I couldn't tell, but he'd had hundreds of years
to recognize another of his kind.

Rhys put down his pencil and snarled, looking
up and muttering a countdown under his breath. In
the light of my glowing hand, his head tilted
upward and his neck stretched, his scar especially
visible. Jagged, with marks where thread had closed
his wound.

My stomach dropped.

"Your scar is on the other side," I said, pointing
to the left side of my neck.

Rhys turned toward me and smiled, giving me a
good look at the unblemished left side of his neck,
then picked up his pencil and went back to work.

"I think you're thinking of mine," said an identical voice from the darkness somewhere behind us.

I swirled on my heel, shining the light of my

220

hand across Broomie and Draven toward a figure that approached from the door leading to the observation deck.

Rhys Aloveius.

The scar leading up his neck to his left ear was especially bright in the vision of my vampire eyes.

Chapter Fifteen

"You..." I whirled around and shone the light over my shoulder.

Rhys was still at work on his puzzles.

"We were expecting you," said the Rhys who was standing. "So I played dead and waited for your arrival. If the braindead idiots couldn't handle you, well, then I thought I should step in." He jutted his chin toward the still-frozen rock throwers.

But I was focused on the double-vision on either side of me. "Twins?" I ventured, remembering Rhys's dry comment about January and August and their "shared burden."

"And the walking dead," added Draven. "The result of the locomotor enchantment."

Locomotor? Why did that word seem familiar? "What, like... zombies?" I offered.

And the lack of blood flow gave that away? It

would have been nice to have thought of these vampire eyes before when I'd been wondering what kind of paranormal presence was on board.

Though there didn't seem to be a way to tell a witch apart from a normie human, even with these eyes.

Left-scar Rhys clutched a puzzle book to his side. "A crude term, especially considering the art required in our reassembly, but yes, that will suffice."

"*You're dead?*" I shrieked. "And you're not vampires or ghosts or…" I waved my glowing hand at the series of frozen giant pallbearers. "What are they?"

Left-scar Rhys chuckled darkly. "Stupidity runs in the blood, I see."

Right-scar Rhys snorted. "Come now. Give her some credit. *She* can talk."

Broomie chirruped indignantly and floated over to my side, settling in my hand that wasn't glowing. Good thing, too, because I had clenched it into a fist and had been about to slug someone.

"What are you talking about?" I asked.

Left-scar Rhys put a hand on his hip. "When I heard that traitorous princess's abomination of a child had *survived* and been *felt* across the distance a few weeks back, I was only too glad to have been brought into service again."

"Speak for yourself, Rhys," muttered Right-scar Rhys.

"Thank you, Miles, you've made your view on

witches quite evident enough already." Left-scar Rhys—the real Rhys, apparently—pasted on a smile that seemed to be barely containing his rage.

"What do you mean, 'princess'?" Draven asked, but the rest of us ignored him.

"You're working with the witches!" I gasped. "You controlled these men—you killed Bedwyr! But then, why… If Lien was a witch… If she was one of them… all along…"

Rhys *tsked*. "Blubbering. Clearly, the golem blood had an effect on her brain."

They knew who I was—they knew about my bloodline.

And this Rhys, the one in front of me, *hated* me for it.

I stumbled backward, tripping over the open suitcase behind me and tumbling inside. I realized as I slunk into it, my legs dangling out, that one brother could have folded himself inside here and just barely fit to board the train.

If he were a contortionist. Or unconcerned about breaking bones and organs. As a zombie might have been.

But why? Why not board the train as a pair of identical twins? It wasn't that out of the ordinary.

"You were supposed to be distracted by the crossword puzzle event," Miles explained, not once ending the ceaseless stirring of his writing implement. "Turns out we needn't have even bothered with that. No one counted on your attention being so captivated by a family of normies. They were entirely innocent of this affair. A stroke of fortune shining on our cause."

I swallowed. The Grimms?

Draven shifted to help me to my feet, then kept an arm wrapped protectively around me, directing our backs to the wall so we could keep an eye on both zombie brothers equally. I gently pushed a hand against his chest once I'd steadied on my feet to put some space between us.

Still, it felt good to have a friend here as my horror roiled my stomach.

"One of you broke into the roomettes," I said. "How? Why?"

Rhys wriggled his eyebrow. "That was my brother. I was at work on crosswords in the dining car during the theft, to establish our alibi. The witches went ahead of him to cast enchantments on all of the doors to unlock them."

Bananaberries. I'd seen three women wandering the halls before the thefts—and I'd fallen for their ruse about getting lost on the way to the dining car.

"But you stole from the Grimms," I said. "And… the witches?"

I hoped they would confirm my burgeoning suspicion about Dora, Sally, and Mabel.

"Some thefts were just to hide our true objective," said Rhys. He didn't *deny* the women were the witches.

Miles *tsked.* "Though *actually* taking that witch's

potion instead of just rummaging around in their car to make it look like something had been stolen was my own little form of revenge. I didn't know what they intended to use it for, but anything to throw a little wrench into their plans."

"Oh, you admit it now? I suppose that explains this, does it?" Rhys opened up his puzzle book and drew out a piece of paper. The event puzzle. The false one. "They left a message for us in a puzzle. *Give back potion or both die.*"

Miles didn't respond.

"Both of... you?" I guessed. The message had been for them, then?

"That was what *I* took it to mean," answered Rhys.

Of course. A witch had disguised herself as me to deliver it. Why show up looking like me if the message was *for* me? Though... why show up as me at all? "January insisted *I* left those puzzles in the dining car," I said, hoping they'd correct me.

Miles cocked an eyebrow. "Who?"

"The little girl." Leave it to these brothers not to pick up on a detail like the child's name.

"Hmm," said Rhys. For just a moment, his eyes flicked over to me. "I could see how one would mix the two of you up. Though you keep your hair longer. Like your mother did." His lip curled.

So the witch hadn't been disguising herself like Eithne had disguised herself as Bette just to make a show of me putting those false puzzles on Bedwyr's briefcase.

She'd just shown up as herself.

My grandmother was here, with the witches on this train.

"Why did you take something from them?" Rhys snapped, his attention back on his brother. "What were you thinking?"

"Frankly, brother, you should thank me for doing so," said Miles, not looking up from his puzzle book.

"Do you see what I'm dealing with here?" asked Rhys, pleading toward me as if I'd feel any sympathy at all. He stared daggers at his brother. "Don't make them angry at you!"

"I didn't *ask* her to bring me back to life," said Miles.

"Neither did I," said Rhys.

Miles stopped writing just long enough to narrow his eyes on his twin. "It wasn't *I* who married the witch queen."

"Witch *queen*?" asked Draven.

I whispered under my breath, about to give Draven the bare minimum detail, minus the whole "I'm a princess" thing. "The witch queen—"

"Keep her title out of your dirty little mouth," said Rhys. "*Murderer.*"

Murderer? I… The realization made my limbs feel like lead, but I fought to keep my grip on Broomie. I *had* killed. Eithne.

How much did he know?

More importantly, *who* were they?

"My mother told me you can't bring the dead back to life!" I insisted, fishing for a better explanation. "Not unless as a vampire or ghost. I wouldn't dare attempt such a thing—"

"Well, you're not *half* the witch my daughter is!" Rhys said. "And I'd hardly call this *life*. It only worked in my brother's and my case because we could split the burden."

"The burden," said Draven. "The locomotor enchantment curse. If assembled back together, the bones of the undead may walk and talk again, but they must never stop performing a task set by the witch who performed the enchantment. Practically useless, unless a witch is looking for a zombie decoration."

"It is not true that we must *never* stop," corrected Rhys. "We have ten seconds before we fall apart entirely. And only one of us has to be doing a puzzle at any given time."

"That's because that burden is shared when it's twins," Miles said, his pencil moving fast. "Because my *dear brother* took it upon himself to father a child with a witch, the queen of witches at that, my entire life—my death—has been tied up with his. And now, even my undeath." He shook his head. "Solving crosswords, solving crosswords, even when stuffed into a suitcase, solving crosswords."

"Will someone *please* tell me why you are talking about a witch *queen*?" asked Draven.

He was focusing on the wrong thing entirely. Still, did that mean the vampires on the whole were unaware of witch royalty?

Me, I was putting it all together. Rhys had fathered a daughter with the witch queen. That daughter, as far as I knew, had to be either my mom or Eithne.

I *hoped* he wasn't my grandfather.

"Yes, well, you could see the *uses* of a shared burden to a witch, can't you?" Rhys barked. "Killing us both at once, tying us together for just such on occasion. The crossword puzzle being the burden, well, that was just Isa's private joke, you see. She always called me a puzzle, an impossible *normie* to figure out. She didn't really like my way with *words*, either."

"Thus why she chased you back to Ireland and took another man for a stallion," said Miles.

Eithne's father. Somehow, I'd known that to be true. There was none of my mom in this man.

"Allaway," I said, my jaw growing slack. Eithne's father's family name. "*Wallaya.*"

"Up, down, scrambled, back," said Miles, the corner of his lip curling into a smile. "A literal crossword. That was my idea. I thought introducing ourselves with the same last name would be too obvious."

"*I* preferred the idea of using the older form of our name, Aloveius," said Rhys.

"And we had to *mispronounce* it to make it less recognizable." Miles shook his head. "Thus the compromise. You're so *good* at that. Just like how you and your witch wife *compromised* by her not killing you on her second wedding day and just sending you home with your tail between your legs."

Rhys clenched his jaw. "I knew from the start that no witch queen had multiple daughters with the same man. They like to see what new bloodlines can do to the family. And my replacement has hardly proven himself as *useful* as me, now, has he? Why, if she had him torn into pieces and stitched him back together, he'd have no twin to share the burden with and he'd be no help at all."

"Lucky me," said Miles.

"Do be quiet. This is about my *daughter*!" Rhys pointed an accusatory finger at me. "Isa lost track of her second child years ago, but Eithne… She did not stop feeling *our* daughter until last month! Now you, you *abomination*, you murderer, you are the last in Isa's direct line of succession? I refuse to believe it!" He stepped forward, shaking me by the shoulder, causing Draven to hiss and Broomie to start whacking Rhys with her brush head.

He wasn't daunted, though Broomie succeeded in getting him to take a step back. "Did you kill her? *How*?"

"Easy," said Miles. "She's no different from your

own child. She sought more power to take down the witch quee—"

"Quiet," barked Rhys. "Do not besmirch my daughter. They may be as dumb as rocks, but the gargoyle golems *can* hear, you know."

More power? To take down… the queen?

Rhys took a few steps back, straightening his jacket with his one free hand.

My gaze darted over the still shapes in the darkness. *These* were gargoyles? But they looked human.

I didn't know what I'd expected. I'd pictured my father as a man made of stone, perhaps.

"I don't care," said Miles. "If Eithne is dead, *she's* next in line to the throne. She and her filthy stone blood." He actually seemed to be smiling at that.

"Even Isa would prefer that her sister or niece ascend the throne than *you*, you filthy abomination!" Rhys towered over me, and if he were able to produce spittle, I wondered if it would be flying. I realized that the man had also never eaten or drunk anything—that the scone I'd seen under his table had been tossed aside to give the appearance of him having been more human. I'd found it on the floor myself.

Oh, why hadn't I ever tried vampire eyes before this? You'd think, at some point, my vampire ex-boyfriend would have mentioned he *literally saw the blood* running through living creatures' veins.

"*Enough*," snapped Draven. Defending my

honor. But I didn't care what this monster called me.

"What about Lien and Bedwyr?" I asked, my mind swirling to the two I'd found in the trunk. "One of you framed Bedwyr for the thefts and put the things you had stolen into his briefcase. If the stolen brooch was a distraction and the stolen potion was not part of the witches' plan, their true aim…" I gasped. The third thing missing, though I'd been late to realize it was gone. "Was to take my onyx pike!"

"A weapon *my* daughter created for your father to protect her vilely sweet sister." Rhys scowled. "The only problem is, Miles couldn't get the wretched thing away when he searched your compartment."

"I *did* find it," said Miles, still scribbling in his crossword puzzle book. "Invisible in the luggage compartment, which I was free to look around in once that broomstick hid herself away in the toilet."

Broomie moaned quietly beside me and I stroked her brush with my glowing hand. Was that why she'd had me get the pike down from the compartment? Had she been trying to tell me someone had been attempting to steal it? I could tell she was ashamed she hadn't defended the pike, hadn't peeked out from her hiding spot to be able to identify the culprit. But I would've rather she'd stayed safe.

"It was too heavy to spirit way. Isa should have taken that into consideration," Miles snapped.

It *had* been heavy after the attempted theft. So it had still been real then!

"They sent one of *them* after it later," I realized out loud. Yes, I had seen a gargoyle headed into the witches' compartment from the direction of my roomette. They must have made the swap then. My stone-scale arm had had an easier time wielding it, and it had been made for a gargoyle's strength. I just hadn't known it was *Eithne* who'd made it. "They transformed a knitting needle into a decoy and swapped it out."

Rhys arched a brow. "An ounce of intelligence, after all. Since the witches themselves can't stand to touch the thing, and the *rocks* are too stupid to properly guard it, they transformed it into an easier-to-carry dagger and left it with us." Rhys nodded at his brother. "We left it here for safekeeping, in our suitcase."

I checked over my shoulder, washing the suitcase in the glow of my hand. Something glinted in the light, but it wasn't an onyx dagger.

Miles's pencil stopped moving.

"Brother?" Rhys asked. He cried out and clutched his arm.

Then, after a few more seconds, his ear fell off and to the ground, the temple of his glasses left askew.

No blood, no gore, just… fell clean off.

Letting out a gasp, Rhys opened up the puzzle book in his hand and shifted his unblemished silver pen to his other, scribbling away.

Miles stood, the puzzle book he'd been working on clunking to the floor. "Actually, it's not here. *I* swapped the onyx dagger with my letter opener when I told you to plant more evidence in the judge's briefcase."

Sure enough, this identical twin, unlike Rhys, was missing the letter opener handle in his front pocket. Though, perhaps, judging by Rhys's evident horror, its absence was merely for appearance's sake.

Rhys was writing quickly in his crossword puzzle book. "That wasn't part of the plan! I suggested you put the stolen brooch there to frame the man in case the staff was relentless in looking for a suspect, and then you suggested—"

"Planting the rest of the 'stolen items,'" said Miles. "To make the case airtight."

"We had nothing else of value to add," grumbled Rhys.

"Which is why I suggested using my *letter opener* as a decoy." He laughed darkly. "But it was actually the dagger you took back and put in the briefcase."

Could my pike truly have been the letter opener, the dagger, I'd had all of this time? It had felt so familiar in my hand. And it had fallen to the floor somewhere in this very car.

"You lied!" Rhys shouted. "When you told us

Lien had only just tonight revealed to you that she'd betrayed us—"

"Yes, I lied. And you never noticed our conspiracy, never doubted either Lien or I. Too busy brown-nosing the witch queen, even after what she did to you. To us. But what would you care what she had done to *me?*" His nostrils flared. "See, Lien spoke with me privately last week while you were with your queen and told me about her own countermeasures. She wanted to stop Isa from stealing the onyx spear and ending her progeny during the ride."

Draven and I exchanged a glance. So he'd been right that I'd been in danger all along. I wasn't going to hear the end of this. "REGGAD, EMOC," I said under my breath with a little gesture of my wrist. Unfortunately, Rhys spotted the movement of my glowing hand. I supposed it was hard not to in the dark.

Still, what could he do? He was busy solving puzzles in his crossword book.

The dagger soared into my grasp and I held it up. It was heavy, but not unwieldly. The witches had refined Eithne's design and unknowingly made it easier for *anyone* to use.

"Blast it, Miles!" said Rhys, his pen scribbling away.

"Lien didn't want her cousin's child to be killed, you see," said Miles. "Or perhaps she simply didn't want the burden of being witch queen herself."

"Dahlia, are you a witch princess?" Draven asked quietly.

"Not now," I answered between clenched teeth.

"She invited that *witch hunter* posing as a Puzzle Society judge," Miles said. "I was to get the onyx pike to her once we'd taken possession of it, and she'd pass it along to the witch hunter, who could wield it today and in many days in the future, should he figure out how to lift it for long periods… But I didn't trust the truce she'd made with him for a minute."

Witch hunter? There were such things? And Cable had known one all along.

I was feeling more and more like I never should have left Luna Lane.

"I headed out to switch places with my brother and meet Lien, whom I realized from the start had requested a meeting with me, though she should have known I couldn't rush after her without raising suspicions."

"I *wondered* what she was waiting for," said Rhys.

"You were in the caboose?" I asked Rhys.

"That was where one of us always was," explained Miles, "ready to work on puzzles should we feel the other stop."

"When my brother wasn't stealing things, of course," added Rhys. "Or *conniving* behind my back."

Miles ignored the comment. "I ran into Bedwyr on, of all places, the roof of the train."

"On the roof?" I asked, things clicking into place. Had their footfalls been responsible for the pounding sound I'd heard? "That was how you traded places. One walking above the train—"

"One through the hallways," clarified Rhys. "One or the other working on a puzzle. So no one would see us both at once. When I left Lien in the caboose, I asked her one more time what she was doing there, and she insisted she'd been sent there to lay a trap."

"You didn't think to question *how* she intended to accomplish that." Miles rolled his eyes.

"I did!" Rhys snapped. "She told me she was there to slip our target the sleeping potion without witnesses, and she showed me the tea with the abomination's room number written on it. She uncorked the potion she carried in her bag and dumped it inside the cup in front of me as proof!"

I bristled. *The abomination?* Me?

Miles clicked his tongue. "Yes, what absolute proof. Was she there to deliver the drink to a room or meet the target way at the back of the train? Think harder next time, brother!"

"I'm not used to treachery," said Rhys through clenched teeth.

"You should be," said Miles. "In any case, the would-be witch hunter had, apparently, been snooping around and figured out what I did: You can climb atop the roof without setting off an alarm if you do so from the broken flap Lien prepared between Car 10 and Car 11. I let him know I was onto his little team-up with Lien. She was, after all, among the only people to whom he referred by given name."

Bananaberries! Why hadn't I noticed that earlier? He'd been working with her for the crossword puzzle event, sure, but even so, he'd said himself he only referred to colleagues by their given names. A one-time team-up didn't seem to justify that level of familiarity.

"I told him I was working with Lien as well and pretended to offer him the onyx pike, which he was searching for atop Car 12. He told me he'd witnessed one of those galoots steal from your room." The gargoyles. "So I intimated I was aware of that and that Lien had her orders to take it back and meet me in the caboose. Her insisting on saying she was meeting a colleague other than him before exiting the dining car sold my story—and his fate."

"What do you mean?" I asked.

He arched a brow. "As we made our way toward the back, I tried to get him to admit he planned to kill them all, Lien included. I'd told her it was foolish to rely on him from the start, but she didn't want all of her eggs in one basket, clearly. The man would not say he *wouldn't*. In fact, we'd only made it to the end of the car before he'd made it quite clear that his society didn't allow for the existence of *any* witches."

My blood ran cold at that. Was that why

Bedwyr had shown such an often-keen interest in who I was?

I'd probably slipped up, too, and written "Poplar" on my crossword puzzle. When I'd seen Bedwyr last, he'd been acting more cautious around me. Observant. But maybe he'd known who I really was all along. He hadn't seemed to fall for my "Pop-Pope" surname to begin with.

Maybe writing out my real name had just confirmed to him that was I was the witches' target during the train ride.

But before he could confront me with my own witch-killing weapon, Miles had confronted *him*. "*You* killed him?" I ventured. The blood in the Grimms' roomette.

Miles offered me a particularly pinched expression. "He was a *witch hunter*. If he'd completed his work before I had a chance to complete my objective, well…" He let that sentence go unfinished. "He didn't know about the broken flap I'd made myself between Cars 12 and 13. I shoved him down back into the cars, and we engaged in fisticuffs, wherein I shoved him into the nearest roomette. Unlocked. Even after the theft. Careless. Fortunately, though there was a witness, she was fast asleep and didn't so much as budge when I killed him, making quick work of his carotid artery with my fine-tipped pen." So it *had* been his pen I'd seen in the Grimms' roomette.

"He was woefully unprepared," Miles continued. "Though witch hunters are not known for their frequent successes—they usually start by trying to separate witches from their brooms, then hope to take them unawares—he'd been too reliant on Lien's promise of a new weapon with which to end a witch. He was entirely unarmed. Then again, so was I and I managed to find a way to end him."

My stomach hurt. Even if Bedwyr may have one day been my enemy… He'd been Cable's colleague once, too. Miles spoke of his murder with such callousness.

Then again, I couldn't help but remember how Bedwyr had wanted to take the three elderly women's knitting needles away under the guise of removing all possible cheating aids during the event. And Broomie. He'd wanted me to leave Broomie behind with him.

Had Miles saved me from a confrontation with the witch hunter myself?

"I left him there and made my way back to the caboose to meet Lien and tell her of the, uh, *complications* to her plan, only to find her passed out."

"Passed out?" I said, my mind swirling. I gasped. "The tea. I'd asked her to bring tea to—"

"That uncouth inamorato of yours?"

"*Cable*," I supplied harshly, only familiar with half of what he'd said. Draven grunted beside me. "She poured the potion into the cup to explain herself to Rhys. And Lien sips other people's drinks!"

Miles's shoulder bobbed just slightly. "She must have been nervous. Probably hadn't expected me to take so long to switch places with my brother. Amateur. What excuse could I have given him for the early switch-off that would have gone unquestioned?"

"Apparently, I am so very simpleminded," said Rhys, pressing his pen harder against the puzzle book as he wrote, "I'm surprised you didn't try me."

Miles continued as if his brother hadn't spoken. "It never bothered me since I have no need of refreshment, but yes, I had observed that habit about the penitent witch. She always brought a hot drink to our rendezvous. The more anxious she grew in our meetings, the more she sipped. She must have knocked herself out."

What a foolish mistake to make. Then again, Miles had made her wait so long. She'd been juggling so many plans and she'd drunk other people's drinks right in front of me at least twice.

"Never did think she'd have the mettle to see it through to the end," Miles said. "But I used her mistake and the witch hunter's death to my advantage."

"*How?*" I wondered aloud.

"I waited for a bit," Miles said, turning to me. "I had to rethink how best to meet my goals. When no one appeared to have reported the dead witch hunter, and Lien wasn't waking, I knew I was without an ally. I put her inside the witches' trunk and decided it was better if I went to the witches with the news first. Let them know I was on their side. I sought them out for their help with… disposing of the event puzzle judge. That's where I met up with my brother."

Rhys growled. "And the witches accused you of stealing a bottle of their potion."

"A fair accusation, I'll now admit," said Miles. "But they grew softer when I told them of Lien's treachery and how I'd killed the hunter and put Lien to sleep with her own potion to face their justice when she'd met me for our rendezvous in the caboose." The latter part was a lie, but I could see him using the situation to his advantage when cornered. "It helped me gain their trust."

Rhys snorted even as he kept writing in his book. "I don't think a witch is capable of trust. Not entirely."

Miles stroked his goatee, unmoved. "They may not have believed I'd tricked Lien into drinking the potion, but they seemed more focused on Lien's betrayal than my own by then. After all, they searched me, and the other, stolen potion was not on my person. They didn't want to risk killing a human passenger on the manifest should the potential witness—*still* asleep—in the roomette wake, and they weren't ready to confront you just yet, especially if Lien hadn't succeeded in sedating you. So they had two of their rock men bring the body to the roof and drag it to the caboose that way. They timed their takeover of the train with that moment to pose a distraction, especially necessary after the alarm sounded. The rocks aren't bright. I could have told them about the tears in the corridors for roof access, but one of them just smashed the roomette's window open once given his task."

The two heads. Two of the gargoyles. I *had* figured out it must have been two people. The hump on the figure's side? Perhaps Bedwyr's head if he was carried sideways. Even the third arm might have been any combination of the six arms between them. I hadn't gotten a good look at all.

"While Rhys left with the witches and went to work on puzzles, I supervised the rock men from the interior of the train," said Miles. "And noticed you and your little broomstick when you started diving at them from above. I nearly ran into your human courtesan at one point, too. Fortunately, the tunnel knocked you out, and I managed to get inside the caboose while he was distracted and before staff arrived in the observation car."

So that explained that. But it didn't explain one essential thing.

"Why?" I asked. "Why offer to work with Lien —and double cross her?"

"Oh, I never cared about that," said Miles. "If she hadn't knocked herself out, perhaps I never would have sold her out. I just knew whatever those witches wanted least was the best chance I had at any sort of revenge." He bent down to the open suitcase I'd tumbled into and pulled something out, which he kept clutched in one hand.

"And it seems they want *you* to inherit the throne least of all. So I wanted you to have your pike back so you could put an end to their schemes." He laughed. "Ironic, really. I instructed my brother to put it in the witch hunter's things, where Lien had wanted it all along, but only because I knew the man was dead and *you* were about to find it."

Rhys's hands were trembling as he worked. "You told me it was your letter opener, and I should put it and the empty bottle in the briefcase to direct *her* attention to him!"

"The witches *did* model the pike's transformation after our own family design." Miles patted his empty front pocket. "They look the same, at a glance."

Rhys cursed, but I was a bit slower to connect the dots.

The dagger was clammy in my hand. "The empty bottle he put in Bedwyr's case. That was Lien's sleeping potion."

"Originally meant for you," Miles added. "The empty bottle was in the paper bag Lien brought with her. I just thought the sight of it, should you be smart enough to discover it, might… keep you on your toes at least. Though you've had threats coming at you from every direction." He smiled broadly, his teeth yellowed.

"Dahlia, they cannot fight us both," said Draven. "Not when one is otherwise occupied."

"There's something else I need to know," I said, not taking my eyes off of Miles. "You said you did take another potion from the witches' roomette." I realized now as I remembered the scene of the crime that it made perfect sense one of the gargoyles had shared a room with Sally. They'd been their bodyguards all along. Perhaps they'd known to expect Miles to come to rifle through the witches' things, to make it seem as if the thief had been there, so the burly men had let him make a mess of the roomettes right in front of them. Only they weren't supposed to let him take the potion from that case, and that clearly hadn't been communicated to them.

And to seemingly disappear like the big men had on occasion… I glanced around the dim glow of my hand in the room. The rocks. Was every rock here actually able to transform into a gargoyle?

We were more outnumbered than I'd even imagined. Did Draven realize that?

"Correct," said Miles. He unfurled his hand and revealed a flask.

This one was filled entirely to the brim.

It oozed a shiny green color, vibrant in the dark, possibly due to my vampire eyes.

"Why?" asked Rhys. "Why take that from them? Why make them angry with us?"

"As if they ever intended to let us exist beyond

this train ride," said Miles dryly. "Why else put their threat in a puzzle, brother, instead of searching the caboose to find the potion for themselves once they were so sure I'd taken it? We're merely entertainment for them."

"I think they *did* try to search," I said. "They headed back here to the observation car at one point, but they were stopped by the staff."

"If only they'd deigned to take seats instead of roomettes." Miles chuckled. "Every time one of us were stopped, we just showed them our ticket for Car 28. That let us stay close to the caboose and have an excuse to be walking back and forth in the train."

"That was *my* idea," added Rhys, as if he deserved credit for it.

I ignored him. "Why didn't they just fly above the train?"

"I don't think they were ready to potentially alert you to their presence," offered Miles. "They'd always planned to wait until the middle of the night, when the passengers were sure to be asleep. It'd make the normie sleeping enchantment easier to activate. But that was all for naught when they moved up their timetable to cover up the murder. You were awake, alert, and there was no taking you by surprise anymore if you weren't knocked out with a sleeping potion. An enchantment of that nature is difficult to apply to the paranormal."

Rhys's brow furrowed. "They need us," he said,

likely referring to the witches. "They brought us back to life to accompany them for a reason."

"Their guardians would have sufficed," Miles said. "*Think about it.* She knew if she brought you back and told you what had become of your daughter, you would feel it, the emotional wrenching of your heart more painful than the physical pain we endured when the queen had her guardians tear us both to pieces. Though you *knew* your child had chosen to distance herself from her mother for a reason, you played right into your former wife's hands. Helping her seek vengeance on the witch who killed your child? No. You're helping her get what *she* wants and that's reason enough for me to put a stop to it."

Rhys's lips pinched together.

"It looks like Lien's hope of saving your life may be a foolish one," Miles said. I realized with a start he was talking to *me*. "Which, alas, could mean that wretched queen's victory is assured. But I can at least give you a fighting chance."

"You wouldn't dare." Rhys looked up from the puzzle book, and his pen stopped. Seconds passed.

Miles's left ear fell clean off, his glasses sliding off with it.

Rhys looked quickly to me, his eyes pleading. "Tell me Eithne lives," he said. "Tell me Isa was wrong. That she was lying to me. That you didn't kill her."

I shook my head slowly, unable to contradict him.

The pen slipped from Rhys's hands, followed by the puzzle book, both clattering to the floor.

"Better protect your friends, golem-blooded witch." Uncorking the potion as his right ear joined his left on the floor, Miles scattered the contents.

Draven popped into a bat and I slid on Broomie's back, holding the crook of my arm out for him to huddle in. Broomie took off across the caboose.

"TCETORP!" I shouted, throwing a bubble I hoped would stop whatever was coming our way around us. It extended to the ground, encasing the open trunk hiding Lien and Bedwyr's body.

Then the entire caboose lit up in green, unnatural flames, a great, giant burst of power expanding outward.

Chapter Sixteen

The explosion rocked outward like a shock wave and then faded out quickly, buffeting around the bubble I'd cast over us and then fading into the darkness.

I'd never tried this enchantment in such a circumstance before—and without a potion to boost me. But I could feel my magic growing quiet within me, even with my conical hat, the strain of too much use within a day like an overworked muscle. A muscle that hadn't had enough rest.

The protection bubble—invisible to the eye—faded and Draven popped back into his humanoid form beside me.

Broomie trembled in my hand, moving her broom head aside to nuzzle me.

"We're all in one piece," I told her.

"I cannot say the same for the rest," added Draven, peering over the trunk.

"WOLG," I repeated to make my left hand light up. Even the minor enchantment took a bit of effort, a sign that I wasn't going to be able to use much more magic before I passed out.

The caboose was intact. There were scorch marks along the floor and the walls, almost as if the wood had cracked open and allowed mold and mildew to set in, but the car was otherwise largely undamaged, as if whatever had been in that potion had limited range or power, enough to blast the interior of the caboose around without exploding the entire thing outward. The luggage was all in disarray, half-cracked and covered in soot, scattered across the car.

The zombie twins were nowhere to be found—I didn't want to think of what had become of their bodies, which would have already been weakened whenever one of the twins hadn't been hard at work with their burden curse.

The three gargoyle pallbearers were easier to spot. Their flesh had become stone at some point, perhaps as some sort of instinct in response to the blast, and they were scattered like broken statues.

Only the three of us and the contents of the trunk beside us remained untouched.

Causing even Draven to let out a cry of surprise, Lien popped up from the trunk, sitting upward.

"What happened?" she asked, her large eyes wide as she looked from me to Draven and back.

Whatever had been in that potion had been

enough to wake her from her death-like sleep enchantment as well, even if it hadn't touched her. Perhaps it had been the loud noise alone.

"You tell me," I said, clutching the handle of my onyx dagger at my thigh, not sure if I could use it again, even after everything I'd faced on this train. Broomie nodded and chirruped her agreement. Then she pointed her brush head upward as if sniffing the air and Lien fumbled beside her looking for something before letting out a little yelp.

"Bedwyr!" She shook his body.

"He's dead," I said. "Miles admitted to killing him—after you accidentally drank your own sleeping potion."

"Is that what happened? Rats. Hot drinks soothe me, and I have a habit of drinking them to calm my nerves. Miles killed Bedwyr?"

"He insisted Bedwyr planned to eventually kill you. Me. Any witch he encountered." I waited for her to comment on the fact that I knew she was a witch now, but she didn't.

"I should have known. Stupid idea, teaming up with him…" Lien grimaced and looked around, out at the damaged caboose alit under my "glow" enchantment. "Someone set off the missing putre-faction potion. I'd know my mother's work anywhere. She won't travel without a flask ready to go." With a grunt, she shifted some rocks off of her and leaped out from the trunk to stand on the other side of it. "Where are they?" She whipped out one of the hair sticks from her bun and cried, "MROFSNART!"

The cherrywood hair stick turned into a broomstick, its brush head compromised of messier, more furry-looking bristles than Broomie's, its shaft knotted and bumpy. The broomstick came to life and swiveled its—her—head toward Broomie.

Broomie let out a little gasping chirp, then looked to me, as if to ask, *"Is that possible?"*

Disguising a broomstick at a tenth of its size? I hadn't known it was, but it appeared to be.

The broomstick barked—more like a dog than a cat—and nodded at Broomie, who started shaking in excitement.

"Wait," I told her, but she slipped through my glowing fingers as I grasped for her.

Broomie nudged her brush head against Lien's broomstick, and the broomstick nudged her back. Lien reached up to pat her broomstick's bristles, extending her hand in submission for Broomie to approve before offering her a similar pet.

"Broomhelen," Lien said by way of introduction.

"Broomie!" I shouted. "Come back!"

Broomie let out a moan, started her way back to me, then stopped and swiveled her brush head around again to look at her new friend.

She was trusting enough, clearly.

But I wasn't.

I grew more determined to hold my ground against whatever Lien threw my way as I gripped Broomie in my glowing hand beside me like a staff. Draven seemed to have sensed this as he stepped to my other side and crossed his arms, a silent, brooding bodyguard of sorts.

"Stop this train!" I said. I hadn't been able to, but if Lien had played a hand in creating the problem to begin with…

"I can't." Lien squeezed Broomhelen's shaft tightly. "I would if I could, but my royal blood is diluted."

I blinked. "What are you talking about? Miles told me you were the daughter of the queen's sister—"

"Mabel," Lien said.

A chill went through me. So Mabel was a witch royal. What of Sally and Dora, then? Where was the witch queen hiding?

Lien didn't seem to know what I was thinking, instead spilling out an explanation quickly. "The witch queen is the most powerful witch alive," she said. "Her direct heirs are second-most powerful. Each direct heir dilutes the royal bloodline, and only an heir's death can restore greater power to an offshoot of the royal family."

My brain was scrambling to follow along with what she was saying. So my mother's mother was the supreme witch, basically, and my mother and Eithne had both then been almost as powerful, and then some of that "direct line" power had passed to me.

Only now both my mother and Eithne were dead.

I stared at the dagger in my hand for a moment, as if it could tell me if I was wielding more power than I had been before Eithne's end.

Could it be…?

"But I… I couldn't stop it, either," I whispered.

"You can't wield such power without practice. Without aids," said Lien. "We don't have time for this." She moved so suddenly, I flinched, the dagger trembling out in front of me. But no, she was just headed for the trunk she'd climbed out of, using her free hand to rummage around and pull out the doggy bag.

Despite everything going on, Broomie strained in my grip to see what Lien would produce.

It was another potion flask, the liquid inside a familiar rose color and completely full.

Lien handed it across the trunk toward me. "Drink."

I scoffed. "You have got to be kidding."

Grumbling under her breath, Lien popped the cork and took a swig. Then she handed it to me, three-quarters full. "It's just a power booster."

"I *know* about power boosters," I said, snatching the flask from her. It *looked* like a power boost potion. Smelled like one, too. Whatever it truly was, better I had it in hand than her. "I brew them all the time at home."

"You're going to need it," Lien said, stepping back and looking up.

There was that helicopter sound again. There were no windows in the caboose, and my steadying enchantment was still working, but I could definitely feel we were going fast enough to still be a hot topic on the news.

"They heard the explosion," Lien said, like the media report was the most important thing to consider right now. "Mother wanted to be the one to set it off, in order to dispose of your body—after they'd killed you. Miles was never supposed to have taken that potion from their roomette."

She wasn't talking about the media, was she?

She was talking about the witches.

"Wait, you mean…?" I looked at Draven out of the corner of my eye. "Did you see any helicopters on your way in?"

Draven pursed his lips. "I dodged one's lights just outside of Chicago, but no one's been able to get good video of the train. I worried it might be due to magic."

Of course. These witches were clearly less adverse to being discovered than every other para-normal I'd met, but they weren't entirely obvious about their deeds.

A runaway train *could* be explained away by

mechanical failure if one's imagination couldn't reach for magic, but they wouldn't want anyone witnessing what went on inside—or on top of—the train.

They'd put the normies to sleep rather than have them as witnesses.

Perhaps murdering an entire train of normies would have drawn too much attention to what had happened here, inviting the media's scrutiny of what had gone wrong on this train ride for years rather than months or weeks.

So the other passengers and the staff would live. All this time, I'd thought the entire train had been in danger… But it had just been me.

But why go after me here and not back in Luna Lane, after Eithne's protection shield had dissolved with her death? If not those few days before I'd left town, then once I got back home?

My vampire eyes darted to Draven.

The reason was so I'd have to fight alone.

They hadn't counted on one determined friend putting his life at risk and flying out to meet this train.

Before I could thank him—beg him to leave before the sun rose—the helicopter-like sounds drew closer, the metal of the train groaning above us.

The hatch on the caboose ceiling shot open with a blast of energy, but as I waited for someone to drop down, a crack started forming along the edge of the roof, all the way around, the previous damage from the putrefaction potion making the metal crumble easily like rust. The dim light of the night outside filtered in bit by bit until with a mighty groan, the roof came off the car entirely.

"Get ready!" shouted Lien above the soaring wind.

Draven poofed into his bat form again, and I slid on Broomie's shaft, clutching the onyx dagger and the open flask in one hand awkwardly, just as Lien mounted Broomhelen.

The air pressure shot outward in all directions, pushing Draven, Lien, and me against different wobbly walls of the broken car as three glowing forms descended over the remains of the caboose.

It took me a moment to realize the red veins of energy pumping outward from each descending form was the blood my vampire eyes was sizing up, but there was something *bolder*, something *stronger* about the blood flowing through the figure in the middle.

With the moonlight streaming overhead, my vampire eyes seemed almost a hindrance, my focus so starkly on the pumping blood.

"SEYE YM NRUTER," I said, lifting a shaky hand off of Broomie's back to gesture at my face, the new enchantment replacing the hand's glow.

My muscles strained with the effort of moving the hand, of channeling the magic even as I was suctioned against the wall. Broomie strained to keep us floating, but she couldn't budge more than a foot or so from the wall.

Sally, Mabel, and Dora each floated lower over the open car, looking perfectly poised as the air rushed past us.

I only recognized them by their features, though, because they had shed their old age and looked every bit in the prime of an early middle age.

Sally's complexion was flawless, her short, cropped hair hidden entirely beneath a dark blue conical hat, but she was as tall and graceful as she had been in her disguise. She floated atop a broomstick that was so stiff as to not seem at all alive, a dark brown wood with green pine needles for bristles.

Mabel resembled Lien even more in this more youthful appearance, her white hair now black, her thick glasses gone, but her deep brown eyes just as wide and bulbous as they had been behind the lenses. She had on a yellow conical hat and rode a jagged broomstick of white wood, dotted with black knots and ending in black bristles. The hand not wrapped around her broomstick clutched a thick book to her chest.

It wasn't a dictionary. It looked just like my mother's potions book.

Of course. If they could disguise themselves, disguising a book would have been a simple matter.

Now her threat to bookmark something in the book to use against the conductor later made a lot more sense.

Clearly responsible for the helicopter-like sound

was a multi-headed broomstick whose heads—at least two, but they were moving so fast, I couldn't be sure—whirled around behind the third figure in the center. Dora floated atop the long, long shaft, her fiery red hair cut at an angled bob against her alabaster complexion beneath a dark purple conical hat. Though she was smaller than the other two, the way her eyes narrowed straight at me made it clear she was in charge.

"Isa… dora," I said.

"I'm so pleased you've heard of me." Isadora's voice carried clearly over the burst of wind. "My daughters did their best with you, I see."

Um, no. They hadn't taught me her name at all. That was me putting two and two together.

"But you cannot shine a dirty stone and turn it into gold," said Sally, her nose turned up.

With a grunt, I let the force of the wind plaster me against the wall, Broomie beside me. Perhaps the gale had been augmented by enchantments as much as by the speeding train. It felt like I was fighting against a massive magical energy.

Somehow, I'd managed to hold on to both the dagger and the open flask, though some of the latter's contents had spilled.

"*You*," said Mabel, turning on Lien, who was plastered just like I was against a wall with her own broomstick across the car. "We will deal with you later."

"Not so tough without your potions, are you?"

Lien shouted into the wind. "What good was your habit of always carrying a putrefaction potion with you if it's snatched out from beneath your nose?"

Sally cackled at that. "She has you there, Sister. And leaving guardians to watch over it did little good if you didn't explain to them that the man you told them would be rifling through your trunk was only supposed to make it *look* like something had been stolen."

"Is it my fault I presumed a single one of those numbskulls had an iota of intelligence?" Mabel snapped. "*This* is why I hate to be so far from home!" She waved her potions book around. "How am I to brew my potions if I'm not near my equipment?"

"You can't think on the fly," said Lien, her voice growing louder. "Maybe it's time for a new generation to take over. Too bad you're all *too old* to have any more daughters!"

They didn't *look* too old, but a witch's looks could be deceiving. Eithne had been a couple hundred years old at least.

"TEIUQ," said Mabel, silencing Lien with a wave of her hand.

Lien struggled against the force of the wind, just as Draven struggled in his bat form against the door leading to the observation deck.

"Better a disobedient child than an abomination," said Sally.

"We never *were* able to control our daughters,"

said Isadora, sending Mabel an almost sympathetic look. "And here I'd thought you'd had a much better handle on Lien than I'd had on either of mine."

"Nothing that can't be corrected," Mabel said. "NIAP!" she shouted, lifting her hand off of her broomstick and waving it toward Lien.

Her eyes squeezing together, Lien opened her mouth in what could only be a shriek, though her lips were silent as she thrashed against the wall. Broomhelen whimpered and tried to move against the wind.

My stomach clenched.

Was it possible, then, that Miles had told the truth? That Lien was as close to an ally as I had in this situation, other than—

"What's this? A vampire amidst the humans? Perplexing. He'd be immune to our normie slumber enchantment. But easily remedied." Isadora cocked her head, then whipped out her arm. "TAB, PEELS!"

Draven's little bat head lolled back against the door, and he stopped struggling, though the wind kept him pinned in place.

"No!" I cried.

"We'll grab a wooden stake and deal with him later," said Sally, a wicked grin on her face. "I doubt the record of passengers will include an undead corpse such as he. He wouldn't have been able to board in the sunset."

My gaze darted around to Lien, who let out

another cry of pain as she thrashed, and then I saw it. She purposely pushed a single finger against the force of the wind, pointing at me.

At my hand. I had the onyx dagger and the flask.

And these women had been too sure of themselves to take them from me.

Choosing to trust Lien, I shifted my arm, trying and trying to bring the arm up to my mouth so I could drink the power booster.

But I could only move it an inch.

Isadora laughed. "Potions and onyx blades aren't much good if you can't even use your arm, are they, my sweet, sorry grandchild?"

Gritting my teeth, I fought even harder to move as my pulse sped up. Closing my eyes, I *willed* it, telling myself I *had to*. I had to do this. Not just for me, but for Draven—for everyone on the train—because even though I'd seen evidence that the witches would be inconvenienced if they chose to kill every human here, I couldn't trust their tempers not to overrule them.

At least I had to try *something*.

With a roar, I felt an itching, searing sensation all across my skin.

It started on my left bicep, trailing downward to coat the back of my arm, my forearm, my hand—then back up the other side of the limb and spreading throughout my chest and torso, down to my legs and my other arm, too.

Each centimeter of the itching, searing progression hurt, but I pushed through the pain, my skin growing cold in the blast of wind.

The sensation itched up my neck, covering my face.

My breath stopped.

And for a moment, I was certain I would die.

What I had always thought of as a curse, the progression of my flesh into stone, had come back, and this time, it had taken over my entire body.

Don't fear, a small voice called inside me. *This isn't the end. This is the strength you called on to win the day.*

With a sudden feeling of the wind losing its effect on me, I wiggled one foot and then the other, the movement unusual but not difficult, and then I jumped down.

My feet thudded like boulders against the mildew-stained caboose floor.

I opened my eyes, the process slow, the sound like scraping rocks as the flesh had been replaced with stone.

And I stared up at the three witch royals threatening my friends.

I was a gargoyle.

Chapter Seventeen

sadora laughed, her nose wrinkling as she looked down at me.

Lien stopped crying out in pain, and I wondered if the enchantment had worn off or if the shock of the sight of me was enough to snap her out of it.

Moving my limbs in the wind was easy now, so I brought the flask to my lips and drank, my tongue and lips grinding like flint against stone.

"You expect to drink in your stone form?" Sally asked.

I hadn't thought about that. But nonetheless, the liquid hit my tongue, a rosewater sewage taste I could sense even through the stone, and traveled down my gullet.

I could feel the power radiating out from my core, the lost energy recuperated, a strength in my limbs.

Broomie cooed beside me, brushing her bristles

against me, but I couldn't feel them. Smashing the flask to the ground, I flexed my fingers and listened to my joints crack.

I hadn't been able to move my joints so well when the stone scales had grown over them before.

"ESAEC DNIW!" I said, moving my stone arms toward Lien.

She slid down the wall and to the ground.

"Broomie?" I asked, turning my stone neck with a grinding sound. She seemed to be on the same wavelength, and as I moved my arm to repeat the enchantment on the wind buffeting against Draven, she caught him, tucking the little bat between her bristles and guarding him.

Lien soared on Broomhelen over to me.

The three witches hovering over us seemed stunned, unable to react fast enough.

"KCOR, EMOC!" said Lien, gesturing toward the open trunk full of boulders. One went soaring, landing at our feet.

"Hurry!" she said. "Bring it to life! Only those high up in the royal family can control the golems who are used as guardians."

Was that why those three attacking gargoyles had frozen in place like statues when I'd enchanted them to stop? If it were anyone else I'd commanded, they'd stop what they were doing, but they'd soon be able to move again.

"How?" I asked her. My voice sounded like it was crunching across gravel.

"Close your eyes," she said, casting an enchantment. But she spoke too fast for me to unravel the meaning of it. A burst of energy shot up at the three witches, sending Sally rolling on her broomstick sideways. "And drop the stone skin if you want some levity."

She wanted me to transform out of my stone skin? I didn't know how I'd transformed *into* it to begin with. And the only way I knew to get it to retreat was to kiss Cable.

I didn't have time for the blush I felt soaring to my cheek.

But it was just the reminder of warmth that I needed.

Closing my eyes, I willed my gargoyle blood to retreat, even as I spoke the words I instinctively knew would awaken my protector. "EFIL OT, ELYOGRAG!"

I opened my eyes, not hearing the scrape of stone. My arms in front of me—my right hand still clutching the onyx dagger—were flesh and blood.

I jumped on Broomie's shaft just as the boulder at my feet trembled and glowed into life.

"You want to play that game?" Mabel sneered. Sally had righted herself and flew over toward the open trunk, casting an enchantment under her breath.

"No!" said Lien. "LAES, KNURT!" Her enchantment caused the trunk to snap shut, a glow like molten fire traveling along the seams to make it unable to reopen.

I was already taking to the skies, the air strangely still even as we kept barreling forward.

Kept barreling forward.

We were still on an enchanted train. And I had a power-boosting potion within me.

A new kind of power I didn't fully understand.

And a new sudden *belief* that Lien was right. That—aside from Isadora—maybe I had access to power beyond the rest of them.

"Protect your princess!" Lien shouted before casting an enchantment that shot up a bolt of lightning, sending Mabel and Sally even farther apart. Mabel clutched her potions book tightly to her chest with one hand, even when rocked by the enchantment.

I looked down to find my boulder had grown… into a young boy, no bigger than about the age of seven, covered in stone skin.

"Ha! What a little thing!" Isadora floated around the caboose, the two of us locked in a circle, her broomstick's endless chopping thundering out into the air. "Still need some practice when it comes to creating guardians, I see?"

She had her back to my gargoyle boy, so confident was she that he was not a threat. She whipped her hand high above her. "LLA—"

Before she could finish, I shouted, louder, without Isadora's cool, confident poise but in no need of such a thing. "HGIH PAEL!" I gestured at the stone boy beneath her broom.

My gargoyle boy didn't hesitate, leaping up and sticking his stone hand between the broomstick's blade.

The helicopter sound became a scraping screech, the two brush heads—which seemed to be comprised of sharp, stiff feathers, not bristles—grinding with sparks against his stone fist.

He took hold of one head with the other hand and yanked, pulling the entire broomstick—Isadora included—down.

"TCELFED!" said Lien, spinning to stop a burst of energy from Sally's palms headed for her.

I copied her example. "TCELFED!" I said to a burst of energy shooting from Mabel, sending the crackling lightning-like light away from Lien and straight to Sally.

Sally screamed and rolled, flying off the train and crashing into a line of trees.

She didn't seem to be chasing right back after us.

"You wouldn't *dare*," said Mabel, staring her daughter down. "Not to *me*."

Lien swallowed visibly. "LLAF!"

The sounds of her mother's laughter echoed out into the wind almost as if being told to laugh had been the enchantment and not "fall" backward. "It's in you!" she cried, spinning in circles as she tried to right herself on her flailing broom. "That same darkness you deny—"

"YLF, KOOB!" said Lien, whipping her hand out again.

The potions book in the hand of the older witch went spinning and sputtering to the tracks behind the caboose, and Mabel shrieked, chasing after it. Lien shot another enchantment at the distracted, retreating witch and knocked her off-course, but not before Mabel turned over her shoulder to shoot an enchantment of her own. Whatever the enchantment, it nicked Lien and sent her tumbling back against the door leading to the observation car.

"LLAF!"

I turned my head just in time to see Isadora enchanting Broomie and me to fall. Before I could cast a deflection enchantment, my cheek slammed hard against the caboose floor, the onyx dagger I'd been clutching skittering out from between my fingers.

Isadora walked over and put her high-laced boot heel on the back of my palm. I screamed. Her eyes darted tellingly to the blade just outside of my reach.

"I don't understand how you can touch that," she said, grinding her heel against my bones. "Cinnamon couldn't. It's a tool meant for guardian hands. Only *they* can slay witches, and only at my command."

She was mad, her eyes roving wildly as she stared down at me.

Biting my tongue to hold back another cry, my brain raced over everything I'd learned. The witches had brought the twin zombies along with the gargoyles to handle the onyx pike. Miles had even said they hadn't liked being near the thing.

"Maybe… being part gargoyle… has its advantages." I strained my neck to check on Lien, but she was slumped against the door. Broomie was pinned beneath me, and I squirmed, trying to let her fly with Draven to safety.

"ELDEEN GNITTINK OTNI MROFS-NART!" Isadora called, waving at Broomie below me.

With a yelp, she shrank and I couldn't see her. I just felt the poke of a much smaller stick of wood, the furry little lump of Draven rolling between my knees.

My heart sank.

Isadora ground her heel harder.

"Guess it's not so easy to turn on that stone flesh of yours at will," she whispered harshly, leaning over.

Behind her, her helicopter-like double-headed broomstick was starting up its grinding noise again as my gargoyle boy steadily blocked it with his stony arms. The sparks kept popping against the moon-light night.

"You know, as long as we're alone, and my

sisters are taking their *sweet time* to catch up with us," Isadora said, "maybe I'll let you in on a little secret. Then I'll bring to life one of my gargoyle servants to run you through with your father's own onyx pike."

My left hand grasped out for her ankle, but it was frustratingly out of reach. "POTS!" I shouted, waving my left hand toward her, but she stepped aside smoothly to avoid the enchantment.

"I fully intend to have another daughter," she said. "There is dark magic that can reactivate even a womb six hundred years old," she said, cradling her stomach. "As soon as I pick out the next father…" My stomach curdled at the strange way she spoke of such a thing. "So I have no need for my niece to take your place. Nor really even my own sisters."

She shot a hand toward, I thought, Lien, but her aim was the trunk Lien had sealed shut. "ETAR-GITNISID LAES!"

I couldn't let her bring out a gargoyle to stab me. I couldn't let her win.

I felt alone, my newfound confidence shaken, but I wasn't.

"Put yourselves together, boys," Isadora said with a cackle. "And smash your blood right out of this witch!"

The stone boy stirred at her call, pausing briefly, long enough for the feathery broomstick to whack him in the face. Isadora didn't notice, her focus on the trunk behind me, the sound of rock grinding against rock hard to ignore even with the chaos all around us in this wide-open car.

"No!" I shouted at the stone boy. The thought of him going to Isadora's side was, strangely, too much for me. "Don't let her win!"

Narrowing his steely brow, the stone boy swung out his elbow, cracking it against the dual-headed broomstick. He didn't even know me, but he was fighting to protect me.

Just as Draven, Broomie, and Lien had done.

And they needed me now.

Isadora turned toward the stone boy. "Interesting. You will not obey your queen?" She looked down at me as if I were gum on the sole of her shoe. Which I sort of was at the moment. "He views you as a royal, too," she said. "Fancies himself your guardian. Stones for brains."

She turned back to the stone boy, her brows drawn together, and spoke another enchantment.

"Hide!" I told him, not thinking of an enchantment to use on him, just pleading with him.

He stared at me, slow to react.

Isadora didn't so much as flinch as I spoke to the boy, and I picked up the backward words for "gargoyle" and "shatter" in her enchantment. Willing my gargoyle flesh to my right arm, I poured every ounce of energy I had into the task.

It worked.

My hand turned into rock, Isadora's heel no longer painful to me, no longer much of a weight.

I flicked it aside and she let out a little cry as she tumbled backward, the energy pulsing from her hands flying off-course, resulting in a thunderous crashing sound behind me.

But the cause of that sound didn't matter. The gargoyle boy was unharmed, shrinking down to a boulder before my eyes. I had a single-minded focus.

Would it be enough? Eithne had insisted *love* was necessary to break a witch, to cause her to fall prey to the onyx pike and die.

This woman knew nothing of love, clearly.

Snatching the onyx dagger in my stone hand, I brought it down on Isadora's boot, piercing through the leather and into the floor below.

I supposed a sharp dagger was enough to wound, if not kill.

She shrieked, and the sound was enough to make her feathery dual-headed broomstick pause in its assault to turn its heads toward her, giving my gargoyle boy the opening he needed to jump up and drive his elbow down again, smashing the helicopter broom down.

I whapped my palms flat on the wooden surface of the caboose flooring, one hand still stone, and closed my eyes, channeling everything —*everything*—I had within me.

"WOLS, NIART!" I shrieked, my voice wavering with the words.

It didn't seem to work at first, but I refused to believe that.

I kept willing it, channeling the energy through my hat and to my hands, draining it all, a stream of power even seeming to filter out from Isadora and Lien and straight into me.

With a grinding noise that was shrill in my ear, the train began to slow. Sparks flew out into the night, but I kept telling this train it *had* to slow, slow so much that it would stop, whatever enchantment had been cast before on it.

Isadora opened her mouth and I raised my stone hand just long enough to shout, "TEIUQ," following her sister's example.

Isadora's foot was festering with blood, and I focused on stopping the train, even as the momentum came to a screeching halt. Footfalls thudded across the floor.

Lien spun, swinging Broomhelen, the broomstick's tail end smacking the onyx blade out of Isadora's foot and clear across the remains of the caboose.

"Why?" I mouthed to her.

"It won't work," said Lien. "Not on her. Not now."

Did that have to do with the missing component? Love?

But Isadora didn't stop to thank her. She rushed over to her broomstick, shot an enchantment of wind to send my gargoyle boy flying before mounting its shaft, and took to the skies, the helicopter blade sound clunky, like a gear was stuck between its blades.

She headed down the tracks behind us, disappearing somewhere into the light of the moon just as the train let out one final squeal and came to a stop.

"You weren't ready," Lien said simply, further explaining her choice to let the witch go. Not ready? It wasn't just about love? "And I have a plan to protect and train you until you are."

I wanted to say something, but instead, I collapsed forward, short of breath.

Chapter Eighteen

e'd stopped in a field still a few dozen miles from Chicago, according to Lien. I almost asked what kind of enchantment she'd used to divine such a thing, but she turned around and I saw the glow of her smartphone, probably showing her our GPS coordinates.

Broomie lay curled on my lap, her head up and brushing against my cheek. Lien had transformed her back for me—I'd been too exhausted to try yet another new-to-me enchantment.

"We have to work fast," said Lien, dropping the smartphone into her navy pants pocket. "I'll change the memories of the normies on the train and dissipate the sleeping smog the witch royals cast. The normies should wake soon, and though they'll remember the runaway train, they won't remember anything paranormal about it, or falling asleep like that as a group. I can change their memories so they can even forget anything *odd* about you."

That would come in handy with the Grimm children.

And *I* was the witch with more power than she had?

I gestured a lazy hand at the open trunk. "Bedwyr?"

Lien's mouth grew grim. "You say he'd planned to kill me, too?"

I shrugged listlessly. I was getting woozy. "That's what Miles said. He couldn't let a witch go if he was a witch hunter."

"Blast." Lien chewed on a thumbnail. "We made a deal. I can't go to the hunters for more help in defeating the witch royalty, then, I guess. Not if it endangers you."

Me? What about her? I wanted to ask. But there were other things to worry about.

"I'll make it so they forget the crossword puzzle event, too. We planned it and used enchantments to get me a job on the train and get the conductor to approve the event, make it seem like it was a real thing. It was just an excuse for me to get Bedwyr on the train without being part of the passenger mani-fest, but I told my mother and aunts that it was to give the twins the opportunity to publicly keep up their crossword puzzle burden since one or the other always had to be completing puzzles."

"They didn't suspect you or Bedwyr?" I asked.

"You'd have to ask them that." Lien put her hand on her hip, her lips clamped tightly together for a moment. "I've done my best to keep in their good graces. Until now."

Now Lien was their enemy, too. And the enemy of my enemy…

But something else clicked for me. They'd planned this whole thing from the start. "Let me guess—the black ice on George Washington Bridge was you as well?"

"Aunt Sally, actually. She specializes in little tweaks of the weather. Like my mother and her potions. It was already skirting freezing that day, so it was nothing for her to add some precipitation and make sure it was especially icy before you passed by."

I scoffed, remembering the helicopter sounds and putting two and two together now that I knew what Isadora's broomstick sounded like in flight. "Little tweaks, huh? The kind that cause multiple-car pile-ups? Were the four of you up there, invisible to the naked eye?"

Lien's expression was impassive as she nodded. "If it helps any, I did my best to make sure no one was too injured. Aunt Isadora always said I was too soft, so I knew it wouldn't be unexpected. I did as much as I could get away with."

Like stopping cars from tumbling off the bridge, for starters.

Atop my ankle, the little bat leaning his cheek against me let out a little snore-like squeak. I was about to rouse him with an enchantment, even if I was too tired to move, when my heart jolted. I'd almost forgotten something so important.

"How long until sunrise?" I asked Lien.

She frowned, examining the bat and scooping him up for me. "I'll fly him to Luna Lane extra fast after I finish waking and memory wiping the passengers," she said. My stomach roiled at how easily she tossed out the idea of memory wiping like Eithne had—it had always reeked of dark magic to me. My horror must have been evident on my face, but she misunderstood the source. "We'll make it," she assured me.

That *was* the more important cause of my distress right now regardless. And she was right. It was better that no one remembered anything strange they might have witnessed on this trip. I'd have to voice my objections to the enchantment later.

"You know the way to Luna Lane?" I asked. Foolish question. Of course. She'd visited the pub there.

"It's where I'm headed." She turned on her heel but stopped, pausing to look at me. "I can protect you there."

In Luna Lane…?

I didn't understand.

"Don't forget your gargoyle," she said, nodding

at the boulder where I'd last seen the stone boy. She waved her hand over the caboose and said, "SELYOGRAG, EMOC."

The gargoyle boy's boulder shot up and to her, and she placed it on my lap beside Broomie. Standing, she looked around.

"He's the last one still in one piece," she said softly. "I can't fix the rest—not even Isadora could."

I blinked. There were pieces of stone statues, small, jagged rocks everywhere. The trunk that was still holding Bedwyr's body was turned on its side, empty of any large boulders.

"Isadora was about to unleash an army on you, but the shatter enchantment she wanted to use on your stone guardian backfired and hit the rest of them instead."

"Guardian?" I asked.

"You formed him from stone. Perhaps you were the first to. The royals got a fresh pile of boulders for the trip. They have a hard time keeping the golems around for long."

"Dora—*she* said he views me as royal."

"Of course," said Lien. "You are. Gargoyles listen to anyone with strong royal witch blood, though they tend to just freeze up when one royal's order contradicts another. Only the queen herself can usually override another's command." She gave me a onceover. "Except in the case of a gargoyle forming a particular bond with a princess. I haven't ever been able to achieve such a thing and you pulled it off on your first try." She nodded, as if she liked what she saw. "Of course, him appearing *so small* means you're hardly the most powerful princess. I suppose you didn't know what you were doing. It's a wonder he was humanoid at all." Before I could remark on any of that, Lien waved her arm over the trunk. "YACED!" The trunk started disintegrating, Bedwyr, presumably with it. I looked away and shut my eyes.

"I'll see you soon," added Lien casually, as if she hadn't just disposed of the body of the witch hunter she'd brought onto this train. "As soon as I get your vampire back to his kinfolk, I'll meet up with you again. The other witches should be headed home for now. They were all injured and will need to regroup. They won't like how we humiliated them— but they don't want their secrets discovered, either. Without their enchantment on the train, the media is bound to finally get a good look at what's going on."

I was glad *she* was so confident that these witches weren't about to attack the moment she left me alone.

But I didn't want to argue about it. Even if she was wrong, someone needed to get Draven back home in time, and I was in no shape to do it.

"I can't heal your kind of exhaustion," said Lien simply. "You used a lot of magic today."

"That's fine," I said. "Go." Then a sudden pressing thought hit me. "Cable!"

She winked at me. "I won't mess with his memories, don't you worry. Now guard that boulder and that onyx dagger as if your life depends on them. Because it probably does."

Broomie cooed in response, as if chiming in that I could rely on her, too.

Broomhelen chirruped back and nodded her brush head, then Lien used a "NEPO!" enchantment to open the door to the observation car to begin her work of cleaning up this mess.

My gaze darted over the cracked and moldy caboose.

Well, cleaning up this mess as best as we could.

There was a road about half a mile from where the train had stopped. An empty backroad now cluttered with buses and passengers' friends' and family's vehicles to take us all to Chicago or home as needed.

Helicopters—real ones, this time—flew overhead, trying to get a shot of the straggling runaway train passengers in the early morning light as we walked our way to the road, rescue crew taking the baggage and the passengers in small groups to the road on utility vehicles. The train needed to be repaired before it could be moved, dozens of train routes delayed or otherwise redirected while they dealt with the "mechanical failure" that had led to our dilemma—and had finally destroyed the engine enough to bring the train to a halt.

No one remembered the train stopping, not even the engineer. He'd only rested his eyes for a moment and then he'd woken to find the crisis over.

That was the story going around, anyway.

"You sure you don't want me to hold it?" Cable asked, pointing to the cantaloupe-sized boulder on my lap.

"Him," I said softly. The driver of our vehicle, a hefty man in something like a thermal rescue suit with reflective tape on it, glanced back at me over his shoulder but said nothing.

I still wore my pointed hat. Beneath my shawl, Broomie lay sleeping, her rhythmic snores probably detectible to the driver's ear. In my right hand, now fully flesh, I still clutched the onyx dagger, for all intents and purposes a letter opener to the casual eye.

I didn't fully trust that the witches wouldn't come back to attack me. I had to be ready.

"Okay," said Cable. I still hadn't told him the full story. He'd seen how exhausted I was and had said it could wait.

There was a dusting of snow on the grass between the train and the road, along with a chill in the air, but I had no energy left to warm myself.

The driver pulled up beside another utility

vehicle unloading some luggage into the cargo hold beneath a bus. Behind it stood the Grimms, Odessa glancing into a compact mirror and fussing with her messy hair, the twins staring at me as our driver helped Cable and me disembark.

"Headed to the bus?" he asked.

"Our friends are supposed to be here—" started Cable. "Drat. Mom came with Faine."

"She had to know sometime." I slipped the dagger into my bag and slid it over my shoulder. The weapon was much easier to carry this way.

Unfortunately, my boulder boy still had some heft.

"Here," said Cable, handing me the handle to his rolling suitcase. It was still a bit crooked. I'd forgotten to fix it after the car accident that felt like a lifetime ago.

He held his hands out for the boulder.

Hesitating, I decided to let go and passed him to Cable. "Be gentle," I said, earning me one last quizzical look from the driver.

We headed down the road toward the barricade. Faine bounced on her heels and waved her arm. Meanwhile, a stern expression fixated on us from beneath her pixie-cut white hair, Ingrid crossed her arms as we neared, more intimidating than one might have expected from her short stature.

"What's the first rule of travel safety?" she asked, eyeing the boulder in her son's arms.

Cable winced. "Study the forecast." So he was supposed to have chosen not to travel where there was the potential for black ice?

Did I tell her about the witches meddling with said forecast, to get Cable in the clear?

I would, once I relayed the whole story. Cable's mother seemed to be enjoying making her son shrink just now.

Faine hugged me, patting the lump at my shoulder that she no doubt recognized as Broomie as we pulled away. "Wow. Crazy night, huh?"

"Crazy day," Cable said.

"Crazy life," I added.

That and my grim disposition put an end to that conversation.

Faine took the roller suitcase from me and gave me a side hug as Ingrid finally broke her serious face and wrapped her arms around her son. Since he towered over her, it seemed more like *he* was hugging *her*, but the worry lines etched around his mouth softened at the touch of his mother's arms.

I remembered that feeling.

"Let's go home," she said, as if Luna Lane were that to her, too.

She'd grown up there, I supposed, even if she'd left it all behind to travel the world as a young adult.

"Draven?" I asked Faine. We'd called her to tell her another witch was bringing him home—Cable didn't ask for more details—and Faine had told us about being on her way. She hadn't mentioned Ingrid being along. Probably hadn't wanted to upset Cable too early.

"Grady called right before you got here. Draven's safe in his coffin."

I let out a sigh of relief.

"Who's the new witch?" Faine asked.

"Later," I said, still weighed down by a sort of intangible exhaustion.

"After the holidays," Faine agreed, though I wasn't sure the news could wait that long. Not if Lien was on her way back to meet us.

"What's all this chatter I hear around town about a holiday birthday?" Ingrid perked up as we reached Faine's dark purple minivan.

"Dahlia's birthday is next week," Cable said. "And she didn't see fit to tell me."

My neck flushed as Faine loaded my bag into the side of her vehicle.

"I forgot," I admitted. "I had more exciting things on my mind."

Cable chuckled and Faine took the second bag from Ingrid. We were just about loaded up—Ingrid in the front with Faine, Cable inside with my boulder boy on his lap, when I felt a prickling sensation on the back of my neck.

My arms clutching either side of the open sliding door, I checked over my shoulder.

January and August Grimm had made their way to the barricade, their mother trailing after them quite slowly as she tripped on her overly high heels.

"Aren't you getting on the bus?" I asked them.

January cocked her head, her gaze flitting between my conical witch's hat and the lump over my shoulders. "Are you a witch?"

Were we back to square one? Or had Lien's memory-wiping enchantment not worked entirely on these two?

"There's no such thing as witches," said August, tugging on her arm and looking over his shoulder as their mother called out to them.

But January still stared at me as she turned, her head almost swiveling around like an owl's.

"Dahlia?" asked Faine, starting up the car.

Letting out a little yawning groan, Broomie shifted underneath my shawl, the tip of her brush head shifting aside the material to poke through.

January's eyes widened, but August and their mother weren't looking.

I waved a hand toward the girl. "ENUTROF DOOG." It was a vague enchantment and what little it would offer would wear off within a few hours, but until then, I hoped she and her family could experience some good fortune.

January gasped and I stepped inside the mini-van, sliding the door shut behind me and settling into the seat beside Cable.

"Buckle up," he said.

He didn't have to tell me twice. Broomie slid off

my shoulders and curled up on my lap, as if asking to be strapped in, too.

Faine backed the car up and soon we were riding off down the road, the sun at our backs, the way home before us.

Join the Spooky Games Club in
Vampires and Video Games

If Dahlia Poplar wants to stay safe, she's trapped back in Luna Lane for the foreseeable future. Though she's happy to be home, her boyfriend is moving back to Scotland for good. But even though her own gargoyle blood showed that she and Cable Woodward are endgame, she can't help but worry that the distance will drive them apart.

However, her love life isn't all that's on her mind. With a gargoyle boy to instruct in the ways of the world and a cousin witch she's barely sure she trusts moving in, Dahlia has a crowded house for the first time in years. When the gargoyle starts playing video games with neighborhood children, Dahlia's overjoyed to see him making new friends. When her vampire ex-boyfriend picks up a controller and starts his path toward game addiction, Dahlia is less enthused because Draven is no longer leaving his house at all. And her relationship with Cable might be the root cause.

Now a vampire lord is in town, accusing Draven of a gruesome murder after someone's attempt to create a new vampire went wrong. It's game over for one of Dahlia's dearest friends unless she can level up to become a better sleuth and rescue the undead man from the actual final boss who committed the deed.

Witchy Expo Services Mysteries: Magic, Conventions, and Murder

Witchy Expo Services. We host your convention, expo, or trade show—with a dash of magic!

Set up in a matter of days, our expos can host even the largest of crowds in our witch-run village of Cauldron Cove. We can offer what no other expo planners can: breathtaking illusions, instant teleportation from one end of the center to the other, floating item storage, and all the exceptional, magical touches that will make your event one-of-a-kind. Inquire about Cauldron Cove hosting your next event today by contacting Bernadette Toothaker, award-winning Head Witch General Manager of Witchy Expo Services for eleven decades.

Nimue Toothaker is ecstatic that her world-famous grandmother is about to retire and has chosen her as her successor in the family business. She's only been working on the expos for a few years, but she's confident she has what it takes to lead her fellow witches and warlocks in the business that defines their entire village. Unfortunately, her grandmother's sole condition for Nimue taking the job is that she share the position with her arch rival, an irritating warlock possessed of two minds—quite literally.

First up is Bookshop Con, where indie booksellers from across the nation host authors and sell books to passionate readers. Nimue's grand plans clash with her co-manager's persnickety demands, but their arguments cease to matter when a celebrated author drops dead in the convention center lobby. Nimue suspects murder, but she knows that if she ends the convention prematurely, the magic at work will destroy her beloved hometown. It's a race to catch the killer before they strike again—all while trying to prove she can handle the job she's so desperately always wanted.

About the Author

Amy McNulty is an editor and author of books that run the gamut from YA speculative fiction to contemporary romance. A lifelong fiction fanatic, she fangirls over books, anime, manga, comics, movies, games, and TV shows from her home state of Wisconsin. When not editing her clients' novels, she's busy fulfilling her dream by crafting fantastical worlds of her own.

Sign up for Amy's newsletter to receive news and exclusive information about her current and upcoming projects. Get a free YA romantic sci-fi novelette when you do!

Find her at amymcnulty.com and follow her on social media:

amazon.com/author/amymcnulty

bookbub.com/authors/amy-mcnulty

facebook.com/AmyMcNultyAuthor

twitter.com/mcnultyamy

instagram.com/mcnulty.amy

pinterest.com/authoramymc

Photo Bombed

DARIA WHITE

Bianca Wallace is a work from home mom raising her teenage daughter as a single parent. She's determined to stand on her own two feet in Edenville, Texas after her bitter divorce. When the town's wedding of the year stars her friend as the bride,

Bianca can't wait to celebrate the nuptials. Neither she nor the guests expect a corpse! When the police suspect the bride, Bianca's determined to prove her friend's innocence.

Lamar Sims, the new police detective in Edenville, is investigating the murder case. Bianca's "interference" is not helping, but she won't stop when her friend's freedom is on the line. He makes it clear he wants her to let the police do their job, so she has to find ways around him.

No one in Edenville is safe until the killer is behind bars. Bianca won't let Detective Sims dismiss her hunches. They may have to work together before another dead body shows up.

Worlds Apart

CARMEN WEBSTER BUXTON

Praxiteles Mercouri, known to his friends as Prax, has spent his whole life on the plains of the planet Celadon. He knows nothing of technology; his nomadic people travel in huge wagons pulled by enormous beasts native to Celadon. His culture is based on clans, duty, and obligation.

Rishi Trahn lives on Subidar, a much more populous world with a much higher level of technology. Rishi has inherited her family's very profitable trading company and in checking up on the business, she travels to Celadon. While sightseeing she is able to avert a disaster for Prax's clan. In the ensuing celebration, Rishi overdoes the potent local wine and causes a crisis for the clan she saved. As a result, Prax ends up travelling back to Subidar with her, but he is a man lost in a maze of a foreign culture and unknown technology. Rishi, meanwhile, feels terrible for taking him away from his people. But not so terrible that she wants to send him back.

www.ingramcontent.com/pod-product-compliance
Lightning Source LLC
Chambersburg PA
CBHW061603190726

48288CB00007B/2156

9781952667459